CHILDREN
OF ASH

GW00481338

JAYE WELLS

This is a work of fiction. Names, characters, places, and incidents are either the product of the author's imagination or are used fictitiously. Any resemblance to actual persons, places, or events is coincidental.

Children of Ash

OTHER WORKS BY JAYE WELLS

The Prospero's War Series
Dirty Magic
Cursed Moon
Fire Water (novella)
Deadly Spells

The Sabina Kane Series
Red-Headed Stepchild
The Mage In Black
Violet Tendencies (short story)
Green-Eyed Demon
Silver-Tongued Devil
Blue-Blooded Vamp
Rusted Veins (novella)
Fool's Gold (novella)

Meridian Six Series
Meridian Six
Children of Ash

Other Works
The Uncanny Collection

Jaye Wells Writing as Kate Eden
The Hot Scot
Rebel Child

CHAPTER 1

Matri

The old-timers speak of the before days, when the earth had color. They speak of fresh green grasses, calming blue skies, happy pink petals yearning toward a yellow sun. They talk of a time when humans had the luxury of creating art and daydreaming. But I know better than to listen to their fairy tales; to the fictions conjured by withered old men.

There's no green in the world I know. No blue. No sunny yellow. In fact, there's no sun at all in the Krovgorod labor camp.

The past, the present, the future—everything is gray.

Ashes cling to the air, the sky, the skeletal landscape. They coat my tongue and clog my lungs. Eventually you get used to the acrid taste, gritty texture, and suffocating scent. You become numb to the knowledge that you're consuming death.

I tell the children that the constant rain of ash is a result of the war. I don't mention the war ended a decade ago. The lies fall so easily from my tongue. They have to. The truth would frighten them too much. And if there's one thing the Troika loves more than blood, it's the flavor of terror in the vein.

I'm lying to you even now. Because gray isn't the only color here. In the Troika's world, only one hue is equally revered and feared—the deep red of venous blood.

I used to be a person, but now I am a slave. All humans are. The undead are our masters, and those of us who managed to survive the war are as good as dead.

CHAPTER 2

Zed

I stood before the hunting party, issuing last-minute instructions. Usually no one under the age of twelve was allowed to hunt, but I decided to bring along six-year-old Blue, and eight-year-old Mica, so I could begin training them.

"When the hairs on your neck stand up, you run like hell. Dig?"

Blue nodded enthusiastically. To her, this was a game, like hide and seek. I'd have to keep an eye on her. Mica tipped his chin to acknowledge my words. The solemnity of his expression told me he wouldn't be a problem. Bravo didn't look up from sharpening her knife on a sliver of whetstone. I didn't call her out, because I knew she heard every word. As my second-in-command—and, at sixteen, the second oldest in our camp—she knew how to handle herself in the Badlands.

"Remember, only kill as much as you can carry. Don't waste a big kill unless you know how to get it back to camp. Fill your pockets and whatever else you have with berries, but don't eat any of them until we get back and one of the elders can inspect them."

"Yes, Pa," they mumbled.

I looked out over my wards and tried to feel optimistic. It had been weeks since we'd had a good hunt. Winter was coming and our stores were low. If we didn't have a lucky hunt soon, I was sure I'd lose a good portion of the young ones before full frost.

"Let's head out."

I slipped my tire iron into the rubber belt I'd made out of an old bicycle tire tube. A knife made from a honed toothbrush handle and a length of chain hung from my other hip. As the lead hunter, Bravo carried a quiver of arrows, a bow, and a knife she'd fashioned out of spring steel salvaged from an abandoned car.

The afternoon sky was clear, and the moon was a white ghost low on the horizon. In the distance, small, dark shapes rose against the aching blue sky. A naïve eye might choose to believe they were just birds, but I knew better. Those black wings belonged to the Troika's bat drones. Normally, sight of the robotic spies would cause a cry of alarm to rise up in camp, but they were flying in the other direction.

I tucked a snare into my pack. It reminded me of a night years earlier, back before the war, when my father took me camping. We'd stood together on a bridge over a river whose name I no longer remember. He'd told me that a ring around a full moon meant snow, and how to snare a rabbit using a shoestring. We'd roasted the one we caught on a spit over an open flame. It was the best meal I'd ever eaten. It was also the last one we'd shared. Four days after that trip, the war began. One month later, Dad was dead and I had nothing but the knowledge he'd passed on and a handbook on wilderness survival to keep me alive.

"Zed," Bravo said in a low tone, coming up on my right.

Between the two of us, we protected a band of sixteen youngs, ranging in ages from four to fourteen. They called us Pa and Ma because they didn't know any better; we tried our best to fulfill those roles, even though *we* knew better.

"I think we should split up," she said in a low tone.

I slowed my pace and looked at her. Shadows fell across her face and mixed with the bruises and dirt. "No."

"We'll cover more ground that way—"

I slashed a hand through the air. "It's too risky with the young."

"Shouldn't be taking them anyway," she said under her breath.

I clenched my teeth. Bravo's protest wasn't unexpected or unappreciated, but I was holding firm. Blue was Type AB+; if the Troika took her, she'd be toast. Mica was A+ but he was big for his age and sturdy. He'd be put in a labor camp, which some said was a fate worse than becoming a meal for some high-ranking Troika officer.

"Keep them between us. I'll take the back—you at the front. They can scavenge for berries and grubs while we stalk. If we're fast, we can finish before full dark."

Camp rules—the ones I'd written myself—dictated that every last girl and boy must be inside the cave at full dark or they'd be locked out. No exceptions. At night the Troika's patrols scoured the countryside for rebel camps. According to my intel, they'd been circling closer and closer to our location over the last few days.

Knowing that, I wouldn't normally have allowed a hunting party that close to night, but we were desperate for food. Nighttime was a hunter's kingdom. Vampires weren't the only beings who came out at night. When the sun went down, the world became a buffet—rabbits, raccoons, opossums. Now that most humans were kept behind razor wire and brick, animal populations had exploded, which should have meant easy pickings for us. But the Troika had recently stepped up its campaign against the holdout rebel groups and had begun poisoning rodent dens. We'd lost three from tainted meat before we'd figured out the cause.

———

Recent rains made the air sweet and thick. Wet leaves muffled our footsteps, a blessing considering the untrained feet of the youngs. Blue and Mica scurried like mice between us. Their wide, bright eyes were alert for mushrooms and berries to store in the slings strapped across their chests. Bravo led the way, her bow at the ready. I brought up the rear. We had told the youngs my job was to watch for game, but I was really watching for Troika patrols.

The sun was still above the horizon, but I knew better than to relax. The vamps didn't need full dark to climb from their bunkers. Their allergy to the sun weakened them, but a weak vampire was still twice as strong as a man. The promise of fresh blood would make them ignore any ultraviolet discomfort.

Bravo's fist shot up into the air. Everyone froze. My ears strained against the oppressive silence. Was that my heartbeat or the patter of tiny feet on the forest floor? Hunting had never been my strong suit. My ears weren't strong enough after a bomb took out the hearing in my left ear during the war. But Bravo's ears were as good as any of the night scavengers we hunted. And whatever she'd just heard must have been good, because her stiff form practically vibrated with excitement. Slowly, so as not to make any noise, she lifted both hands to her head and spread her fingers out to mimic antlers.

My chest tightened with hope. A single deer—even a fawn—could feed us for a long time. If we planned it right we could even dry out some of the meat, which would come in handy once the snows arrived and our prey took to ground. The cautious part of me wondered if I should warn her that we'd have trouble carrying the deer back with just the two of us and the youngs. But saliva was already pooling in my mouth at the thought of roasted venison for supper.

I touched Mica's shoulder and motioned for him to kneel. He tugged on Blue's arm and she followed suit. Taking my own knee, I put a finger to my lips to remind them to be absolutely still. Bravo slowly removed an arrow from her quiver and took several fast, light steps to get into position.

I scanned the tree line for movement. Raindrops from the earlier storm danced off leaves. A soft breeze tickled sapling branches. My pulse throbbed behind my eyeballs. But then…there. Was it? *Yes.* The faintest blur of fawn against a green branch. The edge of an antler scraping a trunk. I smelled the musk of wet fur below the green perfume of the forest.

I'd lost visual of Bravo. She blended into the green-and-brown mosaic as if she'd shape-shifted into a tree herself. I held my breath. Any moment she'd—

The arrow flew like a missile through the trees with barely a sound. The deer cried and took off through the forest, but not before I saw the blood bloom on its coat—a bright red spot of hope for my little tribe. We all took off running with Bravo in the lead. Fortunately, the deer didn't make it too far before Bravo's well-aimed arrow did its work. The sound of breaking limbs gave way to a thud as its body dropped to the ground. Bravo's whooping victory cry filled the air as she burst through the foliage to the clearing where the deer fell.

Over my shoulder, I called to the youngs. "Find some large branches—as tall as me."

They scampered off to do my bidding and I went to join Bravo. She stood over the twitching body like the general of a victorious army. "Well done," I said. "Tonight we eat like kings."

She thrust her chin in the air. "And queens."

The deer kicked high one final time and cried out, this time in total surrender. Its body went still in the damp leaves but steam still rose from its gaping mouth. Bravo ripped the arrow from its flesh and wiped the gore on a patch of moss— arrows were too valuable to waste.

The youngs returned, dragging two long branches behind them. I grabbed a length of rope from my backpack and something more valuable than gold—Duct tape. As Bravo and the boy got busy lashing the deer's legs to the branches, I took the girl farther into the forest to scavenge for side dishes for our feast.

I took a deep breath of the clean air. This was the first excuse I'd had to be optimistic in weeks, maybe months. We were well on our way to having supplies to make it through the winter. Once we got the deer dressed and the supplies wrapped up for travel, we'd move on to one of the old ghost towns and find adequate shelter for the snow season. I knew of two towns within a ten-mile radius that had plenty of shelters we could use. The trick was finding one that allowed us to hide during the nightly Troika raids. Shouldn't be more difficult than finding the cave we currently used.

I'd heard stories about some rebels who'd taken refuge in the old subway tunnels of the larger cities. I always shook my head when I heard of those fools. Why would anyone trap themselves in a tunnel without access to the plentiful supplies nature could provide—food, water, shelter, medicine? But I already knew the answer.

Before the war, humans in the first world had lost almost all connection with the natural world, preferring instead to live virtual lives in exchange for convenience and—they believed—relative safety. Little had they known, abdicating hands-on knowledge would eventually be the thing that allowed them to be enslaved.

"Pa!" Blue called. I looked over and her

excited eyes shone in the waning light. Her little pale hand pointed toward something on the ground. A clump of red mushrooms grew on a patch of moss at the base of an old tree. She looked up at me with bright blue doll's eyes. "Can we eat it?"

I pulled out my dog-eared wilderness guide and flipped through to the chapter on mushrooms. "Says here its nickname is *emetic russula*." I pointed to the words on the page that explained the mushroom caused extreme vomiting. Blue's eyes squinted without comprehension. Like most of the youngs, the war had put an end to any hope of literacy or basic schooling. "It says it's poisonous."

Her hopeful expression faded. "Oh."

I patted her on the shoulder. "You were smart to ask first, though."

A little of her smile returned. "Papa—"

"Zed!" I spun around at the panic in Bravo's voice. "Bats!"

The darkening quiet of the woods shattered in an explosion of high-pitched electronic pulses. The sound stabbed at my eardrums, but I scooped Blue up into my arms. "Run!"

Bravo jumped into motion, too, grabbing Mica and pushing him ahead of her. My skull felt as if it might fracture from the noise and my ribs were bruised from my knocking heart. But I didn't stop running. We couldn't return to the cave where we slept or the bats would find the others. Veering the opposite direction, I stumbled through an icy stream toward the decoy camp.

I looked over my shoulder to check on Bravo's progress, but she wasn't there. Blue whimpered in my arms. I turned fully and squinted into the dusky shadows. Had she found a hiding spot?

A scream answered my unspoken question. My heart stuttered. Without thinking, I set Blue on the ground and knelt before her. "Hide. Don't come out no matter what you hear."

Her small hands grasped my shirt. "Don't leave me, Papa."

I gripped her chin between my forefinger and thumb. Not hard, but firm enough to demand attention. "I have to go help the others. If I don't come back, wait until dawn before you return to camp."

She cried, but I ignored it. "Go." I shoved her away. "Hide in the bushes."

After she'd wiggled under a low thatch of hobblebush, I took off back over the creek. It was darker now. No birds sang, no insects chirped, not even the wind dared rattle the leaves. The heavy silence pressed in on me like a weight.

Cold sweat coated my chest in an oily film. Fear threatened to freeze my feet to the dirt. But some part of my mind was blessedly immune to the paralytic effects of panic. Bravo was still out there. The other youngs too.

I forced my feet to move and drew hard on the reservoir of adrenaline pooling in my diaphragm. Low-hanging branches and undergrowth disguised my advance toward the spot I'd last seen Bravo. With each step the silence gained weight and darkened like a shadow. I was almost to my goal when a mechanical whine cut through the black and green like a yellow laser.

I dove behind an ancient tree trunk and peeked around its rough bark. The bats were gone now, and in their place a Troika rover sat like a great parasitic iron insect on the forest floor. The whine I'd heard had been its engine coming to life—preparing to rise into the night like a mosquito with a belly full of fresh blood.

I closed my eyes and cursed. Acid churned in my gut along with the knowledge I wasn't ready to accept—Bravo and the young were on that craft.

A synthetic wind rose as the craft lifted from the earth and into the inky dusk. I opened my eyes to watch it go. My muscles yearned to run, to punch, to fight. But I was alone and armed only with a chain and a small knife. Launching myself at the hovercraft would be like a mouse attacking a hawk.

At least they were alive, I thought. But the idea brought me no comfort.

Were any of us truly alive?

I'd been around long enough to know that the Troika would take Bravo and the youngs directly to a labor camp. Neither had high blood so they would not be taken to a blood camp for exsanguination.

A dark shape in the clearing caught my eye. It took me a moment to realize it was the deer we'd killed earlier. Its eyes were open but vacant. That, I thought, was an honorable death.

What waited for Bravo and the others at the camp was not honorable. The path they were on now was a slow slide into hell. There would be no quick death for my friends. Vampires liked to play with their food.

I glanced toward the deer again, thankful I could no longer see the blood pooled underneath its too-still body.

CHAPTER 3

Bravo

Gray ash coated my skin and lined the interior of my mouth with grit. It mixed with the blood on my palms and the wounds on my arms. After hours trapped in a wooden box with no food or water and the beating that closely followed our arrival at the camp, my arms hung useless at my sides and my legs hurt so much I couldn't walk without a limp.

They'd made me leave Mica at the main building. I'd learned quickly that it was useless to fight the guards. It only gave them an excuse—as if they really needed one—to make me bleed.

After the beating, they laughed as they shaved my head. They laughed as they tattooed my neck with my blood type. They laughed as they hosed me down with frigid water and shoved me into a uniform and too-tight shoes. And through it all, through the shivering and the pain and the fear, I silently vowed to myself that I would survive long enough to watch them burn.

After the intake process, I'd been pushed out into the night and told to report to building number seven, which was one of the women's barracks. Someone there would show me the ropes and tell me where to go at work time.

The avenues and barracks that made up the camp were sun-bright, thanks to tall lights studding the compound. The harsh glow enhanced the uninterrupted grayness of the landscape. The buildings, the bricks making up the tall walls surrounding the compound, and even the prisoners' uniforms were all hopeless, dusty gray.

A cluster of prisoners limped along in front of me. Hard to tell their genders because they were all bald, like me, and their bodies were emaciated past the point of having any curves. Just beyond the barracks two guards watched us approach.

The guard on the right, a male with moon-pale skin and a mean glint in his eyes, licked his lips. A whimper rose from a prisoner as the guard pulled him behind the building. The rest of the group continued walking.

Screams filled the air.

The prisoners continued. No one even glanced in that direction.

The other guard saw me coming and must have spotted the horror on my face because he flashed his fangs at me. "Keep moving."

I lowered my head but cut my eyes to look down the row between the buildings as I passed. The guard bent over the prisoner's neck. Feeble legs kicked the air, but it was like a rabbit fighting a wolf.

I'd never seen a vampire feed from a human, but that wasn't what made bile rise in my throat. No one helped him, including me. Shame and fear made my skin crawl.

The rest of the camp was quiet, which amplified the noises of the struggle. I picked up my pace, but that earned me too much attention from the guards lining the path. Slowing, I attempted to breathe deep to still my racing heart. But doing so only brought more of the choking ash into my mouth. The acrid taste on my tongue, the flavor of charred lives, suffocated me. I jackknifed forward and vomited yellow bile into the gray dirt.

Rough hands grabbed my shoulder. I yelped and fought the hold, believing they belonged to one of the guards.

"Shut up," a voice hissed. "Keep moving."

It took me a moment to realize the face next to mine was female. I couldn't tell her age, but there were permanent frown lines creasing her ashy brown skin. "Contain yourself." Her tone was low and mean, even as her hands helped support my weight.

Wiping the back of my hand across my mouth, I allowed her to help me stand.

"Don't look around. Just walk." She tightened her grip. "One step after another," she whispered. "Just keep moving."

Our feet moved in sync through the gray dirt.

"Hey!" a nearby guard called.

She kept moving, but waved a hand in a nothing-to-see-here motion.

"Oh, it's you." He backed away.

I watched the exchange but couldn't make sense of it. How could an old woman in a work camp have that much influence?

"Who are you?"

"You shouldn't be here." She said this in a tone so low, I wondered if she'd even meant for me to hear it.

My hollow stomach quaked and cramped, as if it couldn't decide whether it was too sick for food or too hungry to worry about being sick.

Before long, she led me to the dark doorway of the building marked with a number seven. I stumbled through the entrance and fell into a support column. The wood felt solid and sure in my hand, and it offered a measure of much-needed equilibrium.

Several dirty faces watched me with blank expressions. It was hard to tell them apart with their identical stubbled heads and hollow, hopeless eyes.

"What is your name?"

Every eye in the room turned toward the woman who'd brought me.

I tried to swallow, but the rawness there mixed with the inescapable dust made the walls of my throat click together dryly. I coughed and tried again. The old woman watched all this without an ounce of pity.

"Bravo."

"When did you arrive?"

"This evening. Can you help me? I came with a child, a boy. They wouldn't tell me what would happen to him—"

"You should be more worried about your own fate, girl," she said. "Not even a full night inside and you're already courting death."

I raised my chin. "No one did anything to help that prisoner."

"That prisoner's name was Joe. He was chosen because he was caught stealing bread." The woman's mouth lifted on one side in a mockery of a smile. "Would intervening have saved him?"

I opened my mouth to argue, but the grave expressions on every face in that room gave me pause. How many times had they seen their friends and family fall under the fang? How many times had they felt helpless to stop it? Was I a fool to think I could save anyone when I was just as trapped as the rest of them? "No," I said. "It wouldn't have saved him, but doing nothing damns us all."

The woman's right brow flicked. "Interesting."

"Who are you?"

"They call me Matri now."

"Can you help me find out where the children are kept?" I didn't bother to hide the desperation in my tone.

"There's no mystery there. All youngs come to me."

My heartbeat picked up pace. "Can you— would you give them a message for me?"

The woman tilted her head. "What's in it for me?"

If she'd punched me in the face I wouldn't have been more surprised. But it was time for me to stop being shocked and start getting smart. "If you tell them that I'll get them out of here, then I promise to take you with me when we go."

A laugh exploded from her thin frame. The other women laughed too, although with less gusto. I let their pitying humor pelt me like rocks. It wasn't the first time I'd been laughed at that day, but I was beyond caring. I needed to keep myself focused on my goal: Stay alive long enough for Mica and me to get away from this place. Nothing else mattered.

"You'll get me out? Sure, doll. You'll be lucky if you're alive come sunrise." Shaking her head as she walked, she headed for the door. "Rachel?"

A woman whose rail-thin body swam in her uniform shuffled forward. She refused to look me in the eye, as if the contact would somehow curse her.

"Show her the ropes," Matri said to Rachel before turning to me. "And you, try not to do anything stupid." She disappeared through the door, but her laughter lingered like a ghost.

CHAPTER 4

Meridian Six

Rabbit ran into the cave. He waved something in the air. "Six! Six!"

I was sitting in front of the fire listening to Icarus and Dare argue over who should take the blame for how low our food stores had gotten. Happy for the excuse to escape their bickering, I rose from my spot to meet the kid. He thrust a rock into my hands. It was heavy and roughly the size of a grapefruit.

Grapefruit? What a strange thing. When was the last time I'd had one of those? Sometimes when I was young, Mom would bring pink ones home from the neighborhood farmers' market and we'd share one together on the fire escape outside the window of our impossibly small kitchen. My mouth watered now, thinking about how the fruit had tasted like sunshine and sugar—sweeter still, because of the company.

"Six?" Rabbit's voice pulled me out of the tunnels of memory and back to the present.

The meager light from the fire gave the air a reddish tinge and each breath was thick with wood smoke. A far cry from the memory of the bright morning with the taste of sunshine on my tongue. "What's this?"

"I found it in the story cave."

The story cave was a spot a few miles away where some of the local rebel troops sometimes left messages for each other. Usually the messages took the form of symbolic graffiti on the rock walls, but the rock he'd handed me was obviously a message as well. On the surface of the rock—it obviously hadn't originated in a cave, because it was tumbled smooth, as if it had spent a good time in water—there was a six-pointed star painted on the surface. Under the star someone had written *ASAP*.

"Saga," I whispered. He was the unofficial leader of the squads of rebels who hid all over the Badlands, trying to evade capture. I hadn't seen him for several months. After the factory explosion we'd pulled off the previous October, we'd all agreed to go to ground for the winter. Our little squad had spent most of the last couple of months in the network of abandoned caves about twenty miles from Saga's bunker, which we called Book Mountain. We could have spent a comfortable winter in there with him, but with the Troika hunting us down, we didn't want to risk all of us being captured together.

So why was he sending for me now?

"What's up?" Icarus called from the fire.

"Saga," Rabbit answered for me. He was so excited his feet were practically levitating off the dirt floor.

Dare's yellow eyes flashed in the firelight. No doubt she was hoping Saga's summons meant she'd see action soon. I wasn't so optimistic, and judging from the grim expression on Icarus's face, he and I were on the same page.

"When do we head out?" Rabbit's voice had deepened over the last lazy few months and he'd grown a couple of inches. His face was losing the roundness of boyhood and sharpening into the angles of early manhood. Even so, his expression was pure kid as he bounced on the balls of his feet. He loved visiting Saga's bunker.

"We need to talk about it first," I said. The kid's expression fell and Dare crossed her arms.

Icarus nodded. "Agreed."

"But why?" Dare asked. "He wouldn't have sent the message unless he needed us. We should head out soon."

I shook my head. "Maybe I should go alone."

"Excuse me?" she said.

"We're low on food, and it'll be easier for one person to evade patrols than all four of us."

"Bullshit," she snapped. "You just want an excuse to run away."

I opened my mouth to argue, but Icarus cut me off. "Enough! We all go or none of us goes." As he spoke, his posture dared me to give him an excuse to back up the command physically. Part of me was stung that they didn't trust me, but the other part of me was ashamed, because they were right.

I threw up my hands. "Fine. We'll leave at first light, then."

Icarus watched me for a moment, as if he suspected a trick. I stared back. Finally, he tipped his chin subtly and turned his back on me to begin instructing Dare and Rabbit on gathering supplies for the trip to Book Mountain.

With all the attention off me, I let my shoulders go slack again. I should have known better than to hope that I'd have a chance at escape. I'd been pretending for so long that I'd almost forgotten how badly I wanted to get the hell away from them. It's not that I wished them any ill, but being drafted into their rebel cause had never been my plan, nor my choice. Like with so many things in my life, I'd been threatened and coerced into cooperation.

I sighed and squeezed the rock in my hand. Sooner or later, I'd have my chance at freedom. I just prayed that the price for that freedom wouldn't be my life.

CHAPTER 5

Zed

We'd been inside Book Mountain so long I no longer knew what day it was. There, underground, I didn't have the moon or the sun to help me track the passing of time. There were only the dimly lit corridors and dirt-walled cells and the gigantic underground silo full of books. At times when the children or I got restless, Saga would repeat his favorite refrain, "Read a book!"

But the youngs and I weren't used to such luxuries. We preferred to sit in a circle and entertain each other with stories we made up. The fact that we lacked a campfire didn't matter much. I sure missed Bravo, though. She always told the best tales. Scary ones were her specialty.

I thought now of all the times I'd lectured her

on toning down the horror. I worried the youngs would be too scared to sleep, and told her that the world was scary enough. She'd always laugh at me and call me a name, like Old Fart or Stick-in-the-Ass.

Why had I wasted so much time lecturing? I'd spent countless hours talking the youngs through lists and lists of rules, in the hopes that if I could just warn them enough they could avoid running into trouble. But where had that gotten me? I'd walked all of us into an ambush. Now Bravo and Mica were gone, and the rest of us were begging for help from an old man who was probably more than half mad.

"Papa," Blue whispered.

We were in the book silo. Saga had disappeared into his cell with a book of maps. His massive dog, Polonius, however, had stayed behind and was allowing the children to pet him. I was lying on the floor, looking over a book of photographs of celebrities taken well before the Blood War. How obscene they all seemed with their egos on display as boldly as their garish makeup and expensive clothes. But oh, how we had adored them.

"Who's she, Papa?" Blue said.

"An actor," I said, looking at the beautiful, vain face. "She played parts in movies."

"What's a movie?"

"A story told in moving pictures. Actors pretended to be characters in those stories."

"They played make-believe?"

I nodded and flipped the page. This picture was of an old actor, a legend, they called him. I had to read the caption to remember his name. "Yes, but they got paid lots of money to do it."

She frowned. "What's money?"

I laughed. Blue had been born after the war to parents who'd managed to escape the city and live among the rebels, until they were caught in a Troika ambush. Toddler Blue had been abandoned by the remaining rebels, who worried about an extra mouth to feed. I'd found her in a cave, half-feral and starved.

"People exchanged money for goods and services. Sort of like how we sometimes trade supplies with other groups we run into."

Her brow creased as she thought this over. "You never play make-believe, do you, Papa?"

I paused. "No, I guess I don't."

She patted me on the shoulder. "Maybe you should try it."

Polonius let out a low growl and leapt off the floor, unseating the youngs who'd been crawling on him. He took a couple of steps toward the door leading to the corridor. His head was low and his ears lay flat against his skull.

A crash sounded somewhere deeper in the caverns. Voices raised.

Polonius took off like a bullet, barking the entire way. I rose quickly and told the children to stay put while I checked out what was happening.

The voices were louder in the corridor, and now I could tell they were not raised in anger, but in excited greeting. I started toward the mouth of the cavern, but hesitated. Saga had told me he was summoning a particular rebel troop to help us get Bravo and the youngs back. I knew nothing about them. I'd had a few experiences with other groups, and the results were mixed. Some maintained their humanity and were happy to help other humans any way they could. But others had become mercenaries and weren't much better than the vampires when it came to monstrous behavior. While I trusted that Saga would not summon monsters to help us, he'd called on the sort of people who could infiltrate a vampire work camp—not a job for sweethearts.

No, I decided, I needed to secure the children before meeting these newcomers. I backtracked to the book silo. Once inside, I hushed the youngs and rounded them up. They fell into a quiet line quickly. Then it was just a matter of getting them down the corridor and into the cell we shared. Luckily, the hall we were down was the opposite direction from the main entrance where Saga was welcoming the rebels. I promised them I'd be back soon, but I needed them to stay quiet until I returned. Satisfied they'd follow orders, I backed out of the room and shut the door behind me.

My heart hammered behind my ribs and my breaths came in shallow bursts. With effort, I pulled air deep into my lungs to calm them. I was nervous, yes, but also excited. After several days cooped up in the bunker, we could finally start making plans to rescue Bravo and Mica. I let out my breath and, with it, a promise.

I will get you both back. I swear my life on it.

CHAPTER SIX

Meridian Six

Saga limped ahead of us into the book silo—a massive round room with floor-to-ceiling bookshelves. Tall ladders rose to staggered catwalks lining the fronts of the shelves. On the floor a massive wooden table was covered in old maps and open books and ink-smeared sheaves of paper. I'd seen all that before though, so my eyes went directly to the stranger.

"Six, this is Zed."

I nodded at him. He tipped his chin. Neither of us spoke, as if aware that being the first to speak would somehow be a defeat.

The calm confidence in his posture hinted at maturity gained by experience, not age. He looked younger than Icarus, who had twenty-eight years under his belt. Closer to my twenty-three, maybe, but younger. The top of his hair was pulled back into a bun and the lower half shaved. Dark circles under his eyes and a tight jaw hinted at trouble— or maybe I was just presuming that last part. No one ever went to Saga because things were peachy.

As I looked him over, he was taking stock of me too. For the first time since my escape from the Troika, I felt conscious of being female. What's worse, I wanted him to like what he saw. I had no patience for this sort of thinking. Saga wouldn't have summoned me to meet this man unless it was a matter of life or death. And judging by the grimness of the man's expression, his problem involved the latter.

"Zed is the leader of a rebel band from the western sectors," Saga said. "Six days ago, a Troika patrol captured two members of his group, including his second-in-command and a child."

Zed didn't say a word. His expression remained unchanged, but I sensed keeping it so took some effort.

"Six days is a long time," Icarus said from behind me.

"He arrived four nights ago with the remaining members of his tribe." Saga motioned toward the corridor, as if to suggest the others were sequestered in another part of the bunker. "In the meantime, I've been sending out feelers to try to track down those taken. And, of course, I had to wait for you to arrive." The rebuke in his tone came through loud and clear.

"Still," Icarus said, "six days is a long time." His implication came through loud and clear—it was too long to hope they'd still be alive.

"Normally, I'd agree with you," Saga said, "but while we were waiting for you to grace us with your presence, I got in contact with a spy within one of the labor camps. I have reason to believe Zed's cohorts are alive."

My head snapped up. "Really?"

"Krovgorod."

The word dropped to the bottom of my stomach like an anchor.

Icarus spoke the words I'd been thinking: "So they're definitely dead."

"They're alive." The sound of Zed's voice affected me in a strange way. There was something in his tone, some emotion I hadn't heard or experienced in ages, but I guessed it was hope. The fact that he dared to hope in our dark world made him either crazy or naïve. Either was a liability—with crazy edging out naïveté in preference. Crazy people could survive in Nachtstadt. Naïve ones didn't.

"Krovgorod, though," Dare said. "It's impossible."

"We all know that it's not," Saga said with a significant look in Icarus's direction.

Icarus didn't make eye contact with Saga.

Instead he looked toward me with an accusing glare, as if I somehow was complicit in this conversation. I didn't react because I knew he needed an easy person to blame.

"Saga, I really hope this conversation isn't headed in the direction I think it is," I said.

The older man didn't have the courtesy to try to look innocent. "I'm afraid you're about to be disappointed, my dear."

Icarus turned and marched out of the room without another word. The fact that he hadn't yelled or thrown anything was a bad sign. Loud Icarus was way less trouble than quiet Icarus.

"I can't believe you're actually suggesting we risk our lives breaking into a camp to save a couple of kids," I said.

"Excuse me?" Zed said.

I sighed. "I'm sorry if that's hard to hear, but the chance of one person escaping Krovgorod is slim to none, much less two weakened prisoners and a rescue party."

He stepped forward, as if propelled by rage. "I'll go by myself then."

"Don't be a fool," Dare said. "You won't make it within a thousand feet of the camp."

"Children," Saga said, raising his voice, "if you'd all kindly shut your mouths, I'd be happy to tell you exactly how this can and will work."

Zed stared at me hard for a few more moments before backing down. I had to give the guy credit for being brave, even if it was likely to get him killed. Still, I wasn't keen on risking my life so he could play hero to a bunch of brats.

"Six, if you would please wipe that bull-headed expression from your face," Saga said.

I relaxed my jaw and went to lean against the wall.

Before Saga could continue, a cry spilled into the book room from the corridor. A child's shout, but I couldn't tell if it was from fear or fun. At first, Zed kept his gaze on Saga, but when three more cries joined the first, he sighed. "I need to go check on them."

Saga nodded. "Please. We'll fill you in once you return."

With that, Zed walked out the door without so much as a parting glance. Once he disappeared, the bunched muscles in my upper back relaxed another fraction.

"Now that he's gone, I can talk plainly," Saga said. The relief in his tone set me on edge. "The truth is he has handed us the perfect opportunity for our next big move against the Troika."

"How is saving some brats a big move?"

He smiled and leaned against the side of Polonius. "It's not, my dear. That is merely the excuse for the mission. The true purpose will be much bigger."

I pushed off the wall and paced toward a bookcase filled with old books Saga called "encyclopedias". He claimed they were quite rare. After humans began relying on the Internet for their information, many threw such reference books in the trash, believing them obsolete. But once the vampires gained control over all the servers and the digitized record of all human history, no one had access to even basic information. Saga had started collecting his enormous library long before the vampires became a threat, and as far as I knew, owned more books than any other being on earth. To me, they were dust collectors, but to Saga, they were as precious as blood to a vampire.

With my back to him, I said, "The mission?"

"Krovgorod is a work camp."

"We already know that," Dare said. After months of living with her, I knew the frustration in her tone wasn't really frustration, but anxiety. She was extremely loyal to Icarus and was torn between learning Saga's plan so she could share it with him and going to comfort him, even though she knew he'd reject it.

"Labor is not all that goes on there." Saga's tone was patient.

I turned around. Something tickled the back of my mind, but before I could snatch it, he continued. "As you'll recall, our little adventure a few months ago put a crimp in the Troika's plans to dispose of humans once they succeeded in creating a synthetic blood formula."

The building we'd destroyed was called "The Factory", but the only thing the Troika had planned to make there was ash from the burning bodies of human prisoners. We'd fought fire with fire and destroyed every brick.

He smiled because he'd hooked my interest. "You remember the name Pontius Morordes?"

"Dr. Death," Dare said. "Icarus said that asshole experimented on the prisoners of Krovgorod."

Saga dipped his head. "Yes. He's also been in charge of creating the formula for synthetic blood."

I held up my hand. "What does this have to do with Zed's friends?"

He was quiet for a moment, as if hoping I'd figure it out on my own. But I was tired from our journey and frustrated with the old man's insistence on drama. When I stayed stubbornly quiet, he finally relented. "Imagine how devastated the Troika would be if the creator of synthetic blood were killed before he'd perfected the product."

I frowned. "How would we manage that?"

"By killing him and blowing up his lab to destroy all his research."

"I'm out."

His expression went slack, as if I'd finally managed to shock him. "What? But I haven't even told you how."

"I don't care how," I said. "No matter how you spin this, it's a suicide mission. I didn't escape the Troika only to put myself right back in their clutches—in a labor camp, no less. Have you heard what they do to regular people there? Imagine what they'd do to me."

Me, the daughter of Alexis Sargosa, leader of the human resistance in the Blood Wars. Me, Meridian Six, who'd been raised by the Troika to be a propaganda piece and blood slave to the top echelon of the vampire directive. Me, the woman who'd escaped the Troika and joined the rebels, even if it was against my will. I wouldn't just be punished, I'd be publicly humiliated and tortured as an example to any other humans who might have thought to rise up against our vampire oppressors. Not to mention that the target was someone called Dr. Death, who had proven he had no qualms about torturing people.

I didn't need to remind them of all of that. They knew all too well who I was and what I'd come to stand for, because they were the reason the rumors had started. It had been Saga and Icarus who decided to use my name to rally the rebels. In the months since they used intel I'd provided to find and blow up a secret factory, Saga had spread the story of Meridian Six, former Troika blood whore who'd struck the first major blow against the vampires. According to him, throughout the winter, other rebel groups had pulled off minor skirmishes and rebellions under the rallying cry, "Red means life!"

Those had been my mother's final words to me. At the time, she'd been telling me to run and find shelter among the Sisters of Crimson, a group of vampire nuns who provided aid to the rebels. But now those words had been twisted to mean something else. As Saga explained it, he was telling all the rebels that the only way to buy their freedom was to make the Troika bleed. He was fond of telling them that "Freedom is a luxury paid for in blood."

And now he was asking me to shed my own blood—to sacrifice my own life—for a cause I didn't believe in in the first place. When the Sisters of Crimson turned me over to the rebels, I had been given a choice—fight or die. So I'd fought, hoping it would buy me my freedom. But as the cause grew, their demands grew more dangerous and freedom slipped further from my grasp.

"Carmina—" Saga began.

I interrupted him. "Stop it." He only called me by the name my mother had given me when he needed to manipulate me. "I said no. I will not walk willingly into a Troika labor camp. Not for you, not for anyone."

Saga drew a breath in through his nose. "You're tired. Perhaps some warm food and a good night's sleep—"

"Will convince me to commit suicide?" I laughed. "Not too fucking likely, Saga."

His left eyelid twitched at my use of profanity, but he managed a paternal expression. "Regardless, we should hold off on this discussion until you're less...brittle. I just ask that tomorrow you give me a chance to lay out the plan before you reject it outright." He stepped toward me and placed a warm hand on my shoulder. "Can you at least do that for me? Just listen?"

The words, the tone, and the expression were crafted in such a way as to subtly remind me of all he'd done for me since I'd escaped. Woven through those words was the reminder that without him and the others I never would have survived the first week of my freedom from the Troika.

But there was something else there. The threat flashed between his words like neon. If I refused, I would be shunned. No shelter offered, no food provided, no protection from the elements or the monsters who hunted us every night. I'd be alone in the world.

"You're right," I said, finally. "I need to rest." And also to think and plan. Tomorrow, if after listening to the scheme I still didn't want any part of it, I'd need to know my next steps. I'd need to prepare for them to try to force me through blackmail or physical violence. "We'll talk about it tomorrow." I tried to summon an apologetic smile, but my lips felt too stiff to pull it off.

He patted my shoulder. "That's a good girl."

I turned to walk away. My legs wanted to run out of the room, but I forced them to walk slowly. On my way past Dare, she caught my eyes. Her yellow irises glinted dangerously with an unspoken threat. No doubt she was hoping I'd refuse again tomorrow so she could unleash hell on me.

I didn't react to her expression. Instead, I simply nodded and tried to look as exhausted as I suddenly felt. I knew it would gain me no sympathy, but maybe it would buy me some time.

CHAPTER 7

Matri

They brought the girl to me just after dawn. The other children were already asleep but when the door burst open, the heavy clomp of boots on wood woke everyone up. Judging from the lift of the girl's chin, her first few days in the camp hadn't damaged her too much.

That was why I'd requested her to be assigned to my bunker. She had a toughness to her that spoke of hard living in the Badlands. But she was sturdy and certainly had plenty of spirit that only begged for a little taming to be truly useful.

She struggled against the guards holding each arm until they tossed her to the ground. I didn't move forward to help. It was safer that way. The boy, Mica, who'd been with me for the last week and a half, tried to come forward, but I grabbed him and pushed him behind me.

"Here's your *helper*," said Judas, placing scornful emphasis on the last word.

Judas wasn't his real name, but it was what all the prisoners called him behind his back. He wanted us all to call him Captain, but we all found ways around it. He wasn't a vampire, but one of the humans who'd betrayed their race to work for the Troika. Since vampires couldn't function in the daylight, they relied on traitors like him to oversee the camp. Meanwhile, the traitors were under constant video surveillance from inside the vampires' underground bunkers. If any of the humans betrayed the Troika during the day, it was a simple matter of unleashing the bat drones to take out and kill them and any other humans not following Troika rules.

"Is she healthy?"

He shrugged and laughed. "Healthy enough."

I looked him in the eye. "We'll need extra rations, and uniforms." The uniform she'd been issued was already in tatters from toiling in the fields every night. The stench of her body odor filled the space between us like a green fog. A bath would be required immediately. Luckily, I had some lye soap I'd traded for from the laundry workers.

The captain laughed at my request. "You'll have what you need. Just be sure your output increases. The doctor will be very disappointed if you do not meet quota."

The threat was useless. I'd lived under constant knowledge that disappointing the good doctor would be very bad for my health as well as the health of the children I protected. "Understood. Now leave us so I can get her working. The children need to be ready to work at sundown."

He watched me for moment with the look I suppose he considered threatening. But I'd survived in that camp too long to take the bait. "Good day, Captain."

He and the other guards turned to go. As he passed the girl, he elbowed her in the ribs. She didn't make a noise. She just curled into herself, like a fist.

I touched her shoulder. She jerked away, as if she expected me to harm her. I smiled. "Relax. You're safe."

Mica broke free and ran to her. She knelt to hug him hard. "Are you okay?" She pulled back to look him over.

"I'm okay. Matri's really nice. She even gives me a candy after—"

"Mica," I said, "please go wash up."

"But, Bravo just—"

I shot him the look I'd perfected over the years. The one that even the naughtiest young couldn't ignore.

Bravo hugged him again. "It's okay. Do as she says. We'll have plenty of time to talk later."

He complied, skipping off to chatter with the other youngs as they went to the buckets at the rear of the bunker. I didn't like that she'd been the one to convince him to follow orders. I'd need to reestablish the pecking order as soon as possible.

I approached her slowly, stopping at a distance that wouldn't threaten. She needed time to adjust. "Welcome."

She frowned and surveyed the two-dozen children gathered around behind me. "Why are you the one in charge of the youngs?"

"They have different work from the rest of the prisoners. The vamps needed an adult to oversee them."

Her eyes narrowed. "What kind of work?"

I waved a hand. "We'll get to all that as soon as you're settled in."

She ignored my implied order that the conversation was over. "Why am I here?" She looked at the young faces surrounding us. "I don't see anyone else my age here."

"You, I will train to take over once my time is done."

Her mouth fell open, but no words came out. Good. We'd have a talk soon enough about how I'd damned her, but for now I needed her to shut the hell up so we could get busy with the work of indoctrinating the youngs into the camp.

"Your new uniform should arrive soon. We have special ones with a patch that identifies us as prisoners with certain privileges." Her brows rose in surprise. I soldiered ahead before more questions came. "In the meantime, I have a spare you may wear."

"Thank you, Matri."

"Thank me by following my orders. If you do a good job, you'll find your time here will be less hellish than it is for other prisoners."

She crossed her arms. "And if I don't do a good job?"

"You will be reassigned to the mines."

Her face paled. No doubt she'd heard the nickname the other prisoners had given the mines.

"You don't want to spend the rest of your life in the Grave, do you, Bravo?"

She shook her head. I rewarded her with a genuine smile. "Good. Run along, dear. We have a lot to do before sundown."

CHAPTER 8

Meridian Six

Children's laughter bounced off the corridor's packed-dirt walls. On my way to my sleeping cell, I paused to listen.

It had been so long since I'd heard such a happy sound. In the barracks where I'd been raised, there had been lots of other children, but very little laughter. Now, I sometimes got to enjoy the gift of Rabbit's giggles, but his voice was already changing into the deep chuckle of an almost-man.

Edging forward, I peeked around the corner into the room where the sound originated. Zed waved his arms to punctuate his animated voice as he told the children a story. The candle in the center of the circle illuminated their faces and made their eyes twinkle with wonder…or was it adoration?

My stomach clenched. Maybe it was my exhaustion or the stress of the conversation with Saga, or maybe it was seeing such unfamiliar innocence in such a dark place, but the scene depressed me. Something like a clenched fist unfurled in my chest and tears rushed to my eyes.

I fell back before any of the children or Zed could see me and ran down the hall to my room. By the time I reached the doorway, the tears fell freely.

Closing the door behind me, I turned to indulge in the privacy of the dark room. But a light flared in the corner—a single match floated through the air, carried by a hand, to light a hunk of wax in a metal holder. Once the wick caught the flame, light illuminated Icarus's scarred face.

Luckily, the meager light didn't extend to my side of the room, charitably leaving me in shadow long enough to swipe at my eyes and nose with my sleeve. Icarus squinted at the sound of sniffling. "You're crying?"

I shook my head. "Not really. Just tired."

He nodded to dismiss the topic. "We need to talk."

"Can it wait?" I'd hoped he'd take the hint and leave me alone. Apparently it was just not my lucky night. Hell, it wasn't my lucky *life*.

He limped forward. With the light behind him, I couldn't see the scars on the side of his face and body, and he looked almost handsome. "Afraid not." He nodded toward the cot and waited until I was settled to pull over a stool for himself.

The dim light and the close quarters created unwanted intimacy. I folded my legs in front of me on the bed to gain some distance.

"What's up?" I sounded brittle, but I was too tired to disguise it.

"We have to talk Saga out of his plan."

I didn't bother asking him how he knew. Despite his dramatic exit from the conversation, I should have known better than to assume he wouldn't eavesdrop.

"I refused."

A lazy laugh escaped his lips. "We both know he'll convince you tomorrow."

"I would have thought you'd love the idea of killing Dr. Death."

"I would if I thought it was possible. Saga means well, but he hasn't been on the inside. Hasn't seen what Dr. Death is capable of. Even if you could get inside and kill him, which is highly unlikely, you'd have no chance of escaping the camp."

"You escaped."

He lifted his ruined left arm. "Barely. And that was just me. You're talking about getting at least two other people out with you." He shook his head to indicate the mere idea was futile at best.

"Look, I already said I'm not interested. There's no point arguing about whether his plan can work."

"Okay, all right." He rubbed the scars on his left forearm with the palm of his good hand. "You can't let him intimidate you."

Now it was my turn to laugh. "That's funny, coming from you."

"What's that supposed to mean?"

"You've done nothing but threaten and coerce me since the moment Sister Agrippa introduced us in the tunnels under the convent."

"You don't get it, do you?"

I shrugged.

"If you die, every hope of defeating the Troika goes with you. Have him send that kid alone, I don't care. But you're not going."

Cold spread from my scalp to my chest. I wasn't sure what I'd been hoping he would say, but telling me the only reason he wanted me alive was for his precious rebellion? For someone so set on saving the human race, he was incredibly mercenary when it came to caring for individuals.

"I get it," I snapped.

He frowned and leaned forward. "Why are you angry with me? I'm trying to save your life."

"No," I said, standing. He had to lean back to get out of my way. "You're trying to save the rebellion." I opened the door. "I'm tired."

He froze and watched me for a few moments, as if I were a riddle he was trying to unravel. Finally, he slapped his hands on his thighs before rising. "Just promise me you'll be strong tomorrow."

I looked him in the eyes as he approached. "I'm always strong, Icarus."

He met my gaze steadily. When he spoke his voice was unexpectedly soft. "I know you are."

With that, he brushed past me and disappeared down the corridor like a ghost.

I slammed the door harder than I'd intended, but it felt so good that I didn't regret it. Using dry fingers, I pinched the wick to snuff out the flame. The bite of pain felt good too.

Plopping onto the cot, I realized Icarus had done me a huge favor. As usual, talking to him made me so angry I forgot to feel sorry for myself.

I settled back against the wall and began to formulate my plan.

CHAPTER 9

Zed

A door slammed down the corridor just after I'd gotten the youngs settled onto their pallets on the floor.

"Pa?" Blue whimpered. She was still panicky after the run-in with the Troika and the loss of Bravo and Mica. I knelt beside her and made the appropriate little soothing sounds. One she'd settled back down, I went to lie on my own thin blanket.

Before the door slammed, I'd heard raised voices. One had been the girl's—the one they called Meridian Six. The other sounded too young to be the old man, so I assumed it had come from the scarred man who'd stalked out of the book room earlier.

I rolled on my side and tried to calm my thoughts, but there would be no sleep for me. That I knew. What I did not know was how I was going to convince the old man to allow me to join the others on the mission.

After I'd left the book silo earlier, I'd snuck back down the corridor to listen to the conversation. I'd missed some of it, but heard the old man say that his real goal wasn't to save Bravo and Mica but to kill someone he'd called Dr. Death. I'd been so angry at the time that I almost stormed into the room, but I'd managed to hold back. It was an argument I'd never have a chance of winning. Instead, I'd retreated back to the cell. While I'd told the youngs silly stories, my mind had been turning the situation over to come up with the solution.

I had to go to the camp with them.

It'd be a hard sell, I knew. First of all, Meridian refused to do the mission. And I'd seen enough of the scarred man's reaction to the mere mention of the camp to know that he'd never make it. The other one—the vampire—wouldn't be able to pose as a prisoner, either. From what I heard, there was a special camp set aside for vampires who betrayed the Troika. If Dare tried to blend into the population at the human work camp, she'd be found out immediately. Which meant the only person who could truly do the mission was Meridian Six. I had to convince her to agree to go to the camp and convince her to take me along for backup.

And if she refused, I'd have to fight until they gave me the information I needed to find the camp by myself.

I rolled over. Maybe I was just delaying the inevitable. The instant the Troika captured Bravo and Mica, I should have just gone into mourning instead of letting hope get ahold of me. There were so many obstacles—each more impossible than the last.

God, I was tired. For ten years, I'd managed to eke out an existence in the hell that our world had become. First on my own, then with Bravo and the youngs. In some ways life had been easier when it was just me to worry about, but it sure had been lonely. Taking care of the youngs wasn't easy, but on quiet nights when one of them would look up at me with a trusting smile or curl their little warm body up to mine, I felt like I had a real purpose beyond just surviving. Knowing it was up to me to protect all those young lives gave me hope because it gave me a purpose.

So how in the hell could I lie there thinking I should give up on them when they needed me most? The idea of Mica at the mercy of those monsters, or Bravo facing down a group of guards to protect the youngs, was unbearable. My stomach burned hot with shame.

I rose from the floor, careful not to wake the children. I needed to move if I was going to puzzle through this. The corridor was dark and cold as I made my way to the book room. Maybe some part of me was hoping that being around all those written ideas and facts might inspire me. The war had wiped out most of the books before I could develop a love of reading, but my father had always had one in hand. Maybe I'd convince Saga to let me borrow one or two when all of this was done—if I survived.

A dim glow came from inside the book silo. I paused at the threshold and looked inside. At the large table in the center of the room, Meridian Six leaned over a large book and read by the light of a single candle.

She looked up just as I was making the decision to back out quietly. I froze, unsure whether she'd be angry or ambivalent about my presence.

"Couldn't sleep?" she said, her voice scratchy with exhaustion.

I shook my head and took a tentative step inside the room. When she didn't tell me to get out or shoot me a disgusted look, I walked the rest of the way to the table. "What are you reading?"

She sighed and tipped back in the chair with her arms behind her head. The movement made the fabric of her shirt tighten across her breasts and a sharp spear of lust stabbed my groin. I cleared my throat and moved behind a stack of books, pretending to read the title of the topmost cover.

"It's a book of poetry."

I looked up quickly. Her expression was too blank to not be a disguise for deeper emotion. "Anything good?"

The corner of her mouth turned up. "Don't understand most of it. But there's this one—" She cut herself off, as if she suddenly realized she'd been about to reveal something she'd rather keep hidden.

"Can I read it?"

She shrugged. "Knock yourself out."

I pulled the book toward me, putting a finger between the pages so I could close the cover and read it. "*The Chicago Poems* by Carl Sandberg," I read aloud. "Never heard of him. Was he famous?"

She shook her head. "Does it matter?" A catch in her voice made me look up. My vision had adjusted to the dark, and now I could finally see an unusual brightness in her eyes—the sheen of tears.

"I guess not," I said. Our eyes locked and held for a few moments, and it felt like something passed between us, but I was too confused and tired and nervous to understand it.

The poem gave me the excuse I needed to back out of that look. I read the poem out loud, haltingly, because it had been too long since I'd read anything out loud to anyone.

They Will Say
Of my city the worst that men will ever say is this:
You took little children away from the sun and the dew,
And the glimmers that played in the grass
under the great sky,
And the reckless rain; you put them between walls
To work, broken and smothered, for bread and wages
To eat dust in their throats and die empty-hearted
For a little handful of pay on a few Saturday nights.

By the time I made it to the end, my voice burned against my throat and my eyes stung. I kept my head down, looking at the words that had unraveled the fragile grip I'd had on my emotions, on my fear. I bit my lip because I was ashamed for her to see me cry.

"Zed," she said softly.

I swallowed hard and nodded, but did not look up.

"I will help you get them back."

The words were said quietly, like a prayer. I didn't dare look up because I knew if I did I would cry like a baby, and I would never be able to look her in the eye again. So I just nodded, closed the book softly, briefly placed a hand on the cover, and walked out of the room.

CHAPTER 10

Bravo

Matri woke me just after dusk. Her face leaned close to mine and her foul breath invaded my nostrils. I tried to shy away, but in the small bunk there was nowhere to hide from the stench of unwashed body and rotten teeth.

"Wake the children," she said. "It's time to work."

I nodded, as much to end the conversation as to comply. Rising as quickly as I could in the cold, I went from bunk to bunk, waking the children. Mica gave me the most problem, but he wasn't yet used to the reverse schedule kept in the camp. In the Badlands, we kept to a typical human schedule—rising early and sleeping not long after dark. But here, we existed at the whims of the vampires, which meant we'd be up all night and expected to grab as much sleep as we could during the day.

Once the youngs were lined up, Matri took over. She paced in front of them like a general inspecting his troops. "Mica will be with me today. The rest of you will be on garden and KP duty."

I raised a hand to ask where she was taking Mica, but she shot me a warning look.

"Stick to your assigned areas. Do not leave unless Bravo, a guard, or I give you permission. You will be given scheduled bathroom breaks. Do not ask to go at any other time. What's the final rule, children?"

All the children, except Mica, who was too new, spoke in unison: "Never let the guards see your fear."

My stomach dropped. Mica's eyes widened. I shook my head, hoping to reassure him.

Matri held up a hand. "Mica, do you understand the rules?" She cocked a brow and held a finger to her ear. Something about her tone and mannerisms made me wonder if she'd been a teacher before the war.

"Yes, Matri," Mica whispered.

She smiled. "Very good, my dear. Listen to me and you will adjust to life here. Ignore me and you will find this place very inhospitable, indeed." She looked at me, as if to let me know that applied to me, as well.

I wasn't sure how anyone could ever adjust to

being imprisoned. I already felt like a caged animal, ready to claw my skin off.

Matri left the children and pulled me aside. "There is a small plot of land behind the intake building. Put half of them to work harvesting potatoes. The other half will be in the kitchens, scrubbing and cooking. There's a vampire there named Magda who will oversee them. Do whatever she says."

Magda turned out to be about as charming as one would expect. She wore the trademark black and red uniform of a Troika guard and ran the kitchen like a colonel. Huge pots of potatoes boiled over large fires. Some of the children were in charge of stirring the cauldrons using huge paddles. The rest were stationed at massive sinks, where they scrubbed potatoes nonstop.

"It's potato day, huh?" I said, trying to make conversation.

Her eyes narrowed, as if she suspected I was making fun of her. "Every day is potato day." The words were delivered in a clipped Slavic accent.

"How do the workers stay strong if they only eat potatoes?"

Magda's right eyelid twitched. I took a step back. "I'll just go see how the gardeners are doing."

As I walked away, she called out, "Train delivers monthly delivery of swine. Miners get meat rations once a week, everyone else eats protein every two weeks. Next train is expected in two days. Until then, potatoes."

I looked over my shoulder. "If you need me I'll be in the garden."

The air was cold outside—a relief after the kitchen's sweltering heat. But my relief was short-lived because the air was thick with ash, and the garden looked more like a graveyard than the source of nourishment.

Ten children spread out over the rows of low plants. Any green in the plants' leaves was obscured by a generous coating of gray. Each child carried a burlap sack across their thin shoulders. As they moved down the rows, they filled the sacks with potatoes that were barely larger than pebbles. Once their bags were full, runners would take the sacks back to the kitchen, and new sacks were brought to the gatherers.

One of the runners was a boy named Ezekiel. From what I'd seen of his interactions with Matri, he was something of a leader among the children. I put his age around ten, which meant he was only a couple of years from being transferred to the mines. His shoulders still had the narrowness of boyhood and his eyes, impossibly large in his skeletal face, were shadowed with a knowledge too old and dark for his young body.

"Everything okay?" I asked, approaching him.

His eyes were on the children farther down the rows. "Yes, ma'am."

"You can call me Bravo." I bent down to try to catch his eyes, but he stared fixedly down the rows. "Ezekiel?"

"Yes, ma'—Bravo," he said, correcting himself quickly.

"Where did Matri take Mica?"

His eyes skittered toward me but quickly moved back to their original position. "The barn."

"Magda said there isn't a shipment of pigs for a couple of days yet. Are there other animals to tend to?"

"You could say that."

Something in his tone made my spine feel like it was crawling with fire ants. "Tell me."

He angled his face to look up at me, as if trying to figure out if I could handle whatever he was going to say. I shook his shoulder to urge him on. Finally, he sighed. "They ain't tending to any animals. They *is* the animals."

I took off running before I made a conscious decision to do so. On some level, I was vaguely aware of Ezekiel's voice shouting after me, telling me to come back. Then, louder voices, more commanding. *Halt! Halt!* I spurred my legs faster, pushing with everything I had toward the gray metal building on the opposite side of the field.

Halfway across, black figures swooped toward me from both sides like crows. Adrenaline spiked, giving me an added burst of speed. I broke out of the rows and across a flat section of dirt. Ahead, two guards were at attention on either side of a wide-open barn door. Along one of the gray corrugated walls, a line of guards stood, obviously waiting to go inside.

Pain exploded in my back. I flew forward and gravel scraped my exposed skin. A heavy weight landed on my back, forcing my face and stomach into the ground. The crows swarmed me. Rough hands were all over me, ripping me off the ground, pulling my limbs and scratching my skin.

I kicked and clawed as much as I was able, but the effort was futile. I couldn't overcome a group of vampires. Especially when the scent of my blood heightened their excitement and their desire to inflict pain. The tide carried me toward the open doors, but before entering, they veered off to the left.

I craned my neck to see inside. Part of my brain tried to fight the urge, afraid of what I might see. But I had to know. Through the open doors, I saw large lights hanging in a room the size of an airplane hangar. A flash of a small white arm lashed to a table. A tube snaking from the vein in the crook of the elbow, sucking blood like a parasite. A tiny face, white and pinched in fear.

A tall male in black hospital scrubs bent over Mica. At the sound of commotion, he looked up from the arm he'd been inspecting. He wore a surgical mask and two black-marble eyes flashed dangerously when he saw me. It was like staring at Death himself.

"Bravo!" Mica screamed.

I fought. I fought with every ounce of strength in my being. But the hands restraining me were too strong. I turned my face up to the dark, ashen sky, and screamed my rage.

CHAPTER 11

Meridian Six

The next morning, I felt as if I'd been flattened by a boulder. Despite my exhaustion, I'd been unable to settle my mind enough to get any significant rest—especially after that moment in the dark with Zed.

Scraping at the crust in my eyes, I cursed and tried to wake up. Today would not be a fun day.

The sound of a child's laughter echoed down the hall. A sharp emotion curled in my gut— envy. Those children had never known safety or the freedom we'd all taken for granted before the war, yet they still managed to find joy in this dark world. I longed for their ignorance.

"Six!" Rabbit called from the doorway.

I jumped and put a hand to my chest to still my skittish heart. "Damn it, kid!"

He cringed. "Oops, sorry. Saga wants everyone in the book room, like now."

I scratched at my head and yawned. "I'll be there in a sec."

"Hey, did you know Zed could juggle?"

I frowned. "Of course not."

"Cool, right?"

I shrugged. "I guess so." That certainly explained the laughter coming from the other room. "Hopefully he's got other, more useful skills up his sleeve."

"Sheesh," Rabbit said, crossing his too-thin arms. "What crawled up your ass?"

I glared.

"Oh, I get it," he said. "You haven't eaten anything yet, right?"

"What makes you say that?"

He shrugged. "You're always kind of bitchy when you're hungry."

"Then why don't you make yourself useful and get me some food?"

He grinned. "I love you too, Six." With that he darted down the hall, calling out greetings to those he passed along the way.

I groaned and pulled myself off the bed. At that point, I'd have traded my left arm for that kid's energy. Unfortunately, I'd need my left arm and all the rest of me to face the coming battle with Icarus and Saga. Because I was about to show them that their favorite puppet had some moves of her own.

Icarus pulled me aside the instant I walked into the room. "Let me do the talking."

I laughed. "I'm more than capable of speaking for myself." I pulled my hand out of his grasp and walked away before he could recover from his shock.

"Six," he hissed. I kept walking.

Dare stood on the far side of the room. She glowered at me, not bothering to hide her anger. Since we'd arrived at Saga's, her attitude had shifted from ambivalence toward me to outright antagonism. I'd thought we'd reached a stalemate of sorts, but I guess she'd found a reason to blame me for the fact she couldn't take part in the mission—if one happened. I turned my back on her, not because I trusted her not to attack, but because I needed her to believe that I wasn't threatened by her.

Zed was standing near the table, spinning a dusty old globe and running his calloused fingers over the outlines of the old countries. That map might as well have appeared in one of Saga's beloved fantasy novels. There were no more borders. The vampires controlled everything. They'd redrawn borders to delineate territories, but the entire world—and every human and vampire therein—was controlled by the Prime.

When he caught me looking at him, Zed nodded. His eyes didn't quite meet mine, and I felt something in my chest thaw. His embarrassment over crying in front of me the night before was endearing, as was his obvious love for the children he protected. He was a sort of anti-Icarus. They both protected those under their care, but appeared to have completely opposite approaches. Having lived under Icarus's glower for so long, I had to wonder if I might enjoy Zed's approach better.

I shook myself mentally. If things went as I'd planned, I wouldn't be under anyone's power or protection anymore. Needing protecting meant you were never truly able to be free, even if the protector was benevolent.

The shuffle of Saga's halting steps came from the corridor. I turned to watch him enter in Polonius's wake. The massive dog made a circuit of the room, sniffing all present to ensure we were all supposed to be there, before he went to lie down across the doorway. Saga took his spot at the table. Before he addressed us, he closed his eyes and breathed in deep, as if the musty scent of paper and old glue filled him with strength.

"Six?" he said, opening his eyes. "Have you made your decision?"

All eyes turned toward me. The weight of those four gazes pressed down on me. Each of the people watching me wanted something different. Icarus wanted me to refuse. Zed wanted me to accept. Saga wanted me to accept under false pretenses. Dare watched me, too, but she just wanted me to get my answer over with so she could be mad at me regardless of which path I chose.

"I thought long and hard last night about our options," I said. "It's clear there are no easy answers here, and no matter which option we choose someone is going to get hurt."

Saga clasped his hands in front of him, the model of patience. But in his eyes, I saw the shadows—the opposite side to his warm protector role. It was the side of him that manipulated all of us into doing his bidding. It was the side that was fully prepared to withdraw any and all aid were we to balk at his demands.

"Compromises must be made," I continued. Saga flicked a brow, and behind me, Dare sighed audibly. "I am prepared to proceed with a plan to infiltrate the camp."

"Six!" Icarus's voice lashed out like a whip. "We talked—"

I slashed a hand through the air. "No, *you* talked. I know you have misgivings and I believe they are justified. However, what kind of humans are we if we don't do everything in our power to save those children? How are we any better than vampires?"

"Not all vampires are monsters," Dare said.

I turned to her. "Don't try to derail this conversation because your ego is bruised." Her eyes flared like she was ready to attack, but I held up my palm and softened my tone. "I'm sorry you aren't able to help inside the camp, but we need you on the outside. You and Icarus will make sure we get out alive."

She looked so confused at my tone and my words that it would have been comical under different circumstances. Her gaze dropped to the floor, but Icarus wasn't done.

"This is asinine! You're going to get yourself killed and then we'll all be dead in the water."

I turned back to him. "Then I will die either way because you will have to kill me to keep me from doing this."

"You've lost your mind," he said. "Tell her, Saga."

"I'm not done," I said. My voice was surprisingly strong sounding, though my hands were trembling.

"Saga," Icarus said again.

The old man looked from Icarus to me and back again. From the corner of my eye, I spied Zed clenching and unclenching his fists, as if he was preparing to fight us all to get his way. Finally, Saga said, "Let her finish."

Icarus opened his mouth, but Saga's death glare shut him down.

"While inside, I will have three goals—to save Zed's people, kill Pontius Morordes, and blow up his lab."

Saga's eyes narrowed with anger. He hadn't wanted this information shared with Zed.

"Who's Pontius Morordes and what lab?" Zed said, as if on cue.

I quickly gave him a run-down of Dr. Death's sins. "If we are going to take the risk of breaking out your friends then we must ensure that our goals are also met. In this case, destroying the Troika's ability to produce synthetic blood."

When I finished speaking, his eyes, which were so recently bashful, turned hard. "And if it comes down to a choice between the goals?"

"I will do everything in my power to avoid having to make that choice."

He watched me for a moment. I met his glare levelly, but inside I was praying to every divine entity I'd ever heard of to help me never have to make that choice.

"Wait," Icarus said, "there's no way in hell we can send you in."

I put my hands on my hips, prepared for him to tell me I wasn't a strong enough leader or that I couldn't hack the mission because I was too weak.

"They'll recognize you."

My hands dropped. "Shit."

"What? Why?" Zed asked.

"Carmina has been the poster child the Troika has used for years to keep the humans in the camps in line. When I was in my camp, there was a massive poster of her hanging over the entrance." He refused to look at me, as if my face suddenly brought back really horrible memories.

My stomach cramped. Icarus never talked about his time in the camps, but that alone meant it was probably worse than I could ever imagine. Back when I was still the Troika's poster girl for obedient humans, they'd taken publicity photos of me in a worker's uniform looking perky for the camera. It sickened me to think that my image now hung over the heads of downtrodden humans to inspire them to work harder.

"Then Icarus will have to lead us." This was from Zed, who didn't know any better.

His words ignited instant responses from the others. Icarus's skin paled and his eyes hardened as he glared at the kid. Dare stepped forward and slightly in front of Icarus, as if to close ranks and protect him. Rabbit rose from the floor and got out of the way, as if he expected Icarus to beat the kid up for the mere suggestion.

"Out of the question." Saga's voice was like a gavel's strike.

"Why?" Zed asked.

"First, Icarus escaped the camps in a particularly memorable way, so they're just as likely to recognize him as they would Carmina."

"And second?" Icarus raised his chin high.

"We can't risk that you'd get in the camps and have some sort of breakdown."

I flinched because it was the truth. Icarus's mouth pressed into a thin line and his gaze sought the floor. Seeing him cowed like that made me wish he would fight. But it was no use. We all knew that going back to the camps would be too much for him. Icarus was stronger than his ruined hand and burn scars might indicate, but emotional trauma was a handicap that even the most physically capable person couldn't escape.

The room fell silent in the wake of Saga's declaration. At first it seemed everyone was waiting for Icarus to argue, but then the mood shifted and it became clear we were all digesting a reality where he didn't.

"I can do it," Dare said finally.

Saga shook his head. "They wouldn't put you in the work camps, dear. Vampires who act out against the Troika are killed on sight." He sighed.

Zed raised his chin. "I'll go alone, then."

"Hey, what about me?" Rabbit said.

Everyone started talking at once, either arguing against Zed leading or Rabbit going—or both. It continued until a loud, sharp whistle cut through the noise. We all looked at Icarus. "Saga is right on all counts. I can't go, Dare isn't the right species, Rabbit is too young, and Zed can't go in alone. That means we must figure out a way to get Six in."

Dare walked over and circled me a couple of times. Her yellow eyes with their vertical pupils moved up and down as she surveyed me like she'd never met me before. Her hand shot out and lifted a section of my hair. "We could dye and cut it."

Saga's brows rose and his lips pursed. "Shaving it off would be better. They'd believe she was a servant or a rebel more that way." He tapped his foot on the ground, ignoring my outraged look. "She'll need a blood tattoo on her neck too."

Cutting off my hair was one thing, but permanently marking my skin was a level of commitment I hadn't been prepared for. When this idea had come up, I figured we'd just steal in, maybe kick a little ass, and get the kids out after setting off an explosion or something. "That's crazy," I said.

Saga ignored me. "We'll mark her with a low-level blood type. It'll help with the disguise. The minute most Troika guards see A neg or B pos, they lose interest." Which was how most humans in the work camps ended up there. Having a less desirable blood type was considered both a blessing and a curse. A blessing because you would never end up the plaything of a vampire with expensive tastes. A curse because not having valuable blood meant you had no worth beyond being a worker drone—an expendable beast of burden.

"But—"

Dare spoke over me. "But what about this face?" She cupped my chin with her fingers. I jerked my face away from her. "We'll have to do something to make her less delicate."

"Hey!"

A dangerous smirk lifted the corners of her mouth, and when she spoke, the empty sockets where her fangs used to sit flashed ominously.

Saga stepped closer. "How do you change a face, though? We can't rely on makeup once she's inside."

"Swelling."

I froze and turned slowly to face Dare. Her yellow eyes glittered with excitement.

"What does that mean?"

"Do it," Saga said. He turned away.

"Wait—" Before I could say the second word, knuckles slammed into my jaw and pain radiated through my face like fire. I stumbled back and fell to my ass.

Dare advanced. Behind her and through the haze of pain blurring my vision, I saw Saga turn away and Icarus smile. "Don't worry," she said in a taunting tone. "I won't leave any permanent damage."

The last thing I remember before the chaos of fists and the barrage of painful blows and the blood, was Dare whispering, "I'm gonna enjoy this," so low the others couldn't hear.

———

When I woke up, my face felt like a slab of tenderized meat. I tried to smack my heavy lips, but the movement made my jaw pulse like an exposed nerve. My eyes were heavy and swollen, but I managed to get them open enough to blink a few times. Once my vision cleared, I finally saw the ring of heads looking down at me. The light was behind them, so shadows obscured the expressions on their faces, but I imagined there was a mix of pity, impatience, and, in the case of Dare, amusement.

"How long was I out?" My voice cracked. I cleared it so I wouldn't sound as weak as I felt.

"About two minutes." This from Dare, who held out a hand to help me up. She didn't sound as entertained as I'd expected her to, but when I rose and saw her face, it was hard to miss the sparkle in her yellow irises.

"And then I gave you a sedative to keep you under for the tattooing," Saga added.

As if his words conjured it, pain shot through the back of my neck. I reached to touch it and my finger encountered a badge over what felt like a burn. "Ow."

Saga looked me over through a monocle. His brows lowered into a frown and he smacked his lips in disgust, as if the fact I could feel pain made him doubt my ability to carry out the mission.

"Well?" I asked. "What's the verdict?"

"You look like hell," Dare said.

She was trying to get a rise out of me, but I wasn't mad. As it happened, I believed she came up with the perfect solution for the problem of my face being so recognizable. But I was in an incredible amount of pain and didn't relish facing down the Troika when I felt like a mass of nerves and bruises.

"Relax," Dare said, misunderstanding my expression. "Even your own mother wouldn't recognize you now."

"I'm so relieved." My sarcastic tone was muddled by my swollen lips.

Saga pulled back and dropped the monocle. "This might just work."

I crossed my arms. The move helped me realize that Dare had been surgical in her attack—only striking my face and not my torso or limbs. The effect left me looking like I'd survived an epic ass-kicking, but really she'd just punched me a few times.

Icarus had been quietly watching from the sidelines ever since I woke up. Now he stepped forward. "Whether they'll recognize her will be a moot point if we can't get them inside the prison."

"That's the easy part." Saga looked way too pleased with himself for my comfort.

Icarus finally lost his patience. "How can you say that? I planned my escape for months and barely made it out alive." He waved his scarred arm.

"Relax, my boy," Saga said. "Escaping prisons is supposed to be hard." He turned and removed a book from the shelf.

"It's almost impossible to bust out of a prison camp, but no one ever expects anyone to break *in*."

CHAPTER 12

Zed

After Meridian Six left the room, I followed her down the corridor. When I called her name, she didn't stop at first. I jogged to catch up, finally reaching her at the door to her room.

I touched her arm, only to have my hand violently knocked away. "Sorry," I said, backing up.

"What do you want?"

Squaring my shoulders, I met her eyes. "I'm going with you."

She laughed and looked at me with pity. "Don't be ridiculous. You're just a kid."

I'd made a horrible mistake asking these people for help. Anger and frustration warred in my gut, but I was determined to make this shitty situation work. It had to, or I'd lose Bravo and

Mica forever. "I'm nineteen. You can't be much older. How long you been living away from the luxury of the Prime's palace?"

Her eyes shied away, but not before I saw the truth.

"I've heard the rumors about you," I said, stepping closer. "Meridian Six, savior of the human race, blew up some horrible place the Troika built near the city. As impressive as that is, those rumors started less than six months ago. Forgive me, sweetheart, but I've been surviving in the Badlands going on a decade. Call me a kid if you want, but I'm a kid who's survived and managed to keep a lot of other people alive in the process. Between the two of us, I have the longer track record of success."

Her chin rose. "Would those two the Troika took three days ago agree with that track record?"

Anger made the muscles in my fist contract. She was baiting me. Trying to get me to lose my cool so she'd have an excuse to cut me out of the mission. "Bait me all you want, but you need me."

"How you figure?"

"I heard what the old man said yesterday. About killing Dr. Death."

Her right eyelid twitched. Clearly she and the others had thought I was out of earshot when they had talked about their true plans. I enjoyed surprising her, but I was looking forward to playing the ace up my sleeve. "Back before the war, my family lived in the mountains around southern Pennsylvania."

"So?"

"So," I said slowly, "my daddy was in the mining business. If the war hadn't happened and forced us to migrate for survival, I would have been a miner too."

"What does that—"

"What it means," I spoke over her, "is I know about explosives. Your plan is to blow up Dr. Death when you light up the lab, right? Kill two birds with one stick of dynamite?"

"Killing Dr. Death can be accomplished without explosives. As for the labs, all I need is a match."

"Or we could make your own explosives once we're inside. Icarus said the main labor at the camp is mining coal. If they don't have explosives there, they'll for sure have the makings of them."

Her mask of indifference slipped a couple of inches. "You know how to make them?"

I nodded with a smile and delivered my knockout. "Besides that, Bravo won't follow your lead unless I'm there."

This was a lie. If things were as bad at the camp as I was expecting, Bravo would do just about anything to protect Mica. But I couldn't afford to let Meridian know that. Truth be, I didn't quite trust her. Saga seemed to think she was the great hope of humanity, but I hadn't seen much yet to prove him right. If the choice came down between rescue or destroying the Troika power source, she'd abandon Bravo and the others in a heartbeat. I needed to be there to be sure that choice wasn't made.

When she finally spoke, she looked less defeated than resigned. "I'll have to talk to the others."

I crossed my arms. "You have to get their permission, you mean."

Ever since I'd arrived, I'd heard a lot of talk about Meridian being the savior, but I'd yet to see her make a decision without Saga's or Icarus's go ahead. She might have what it took to lead, but I hadn't seen evidence of that beyond propaganda. Yet another reason to ensure I went with her. Every mission needed a leader. I couldn't chance so much on someone who was little more than a puppet for an old man and a bitter cripple.

Her eyes narrowed and she stepped into my space. "Watch yourself. You came to us for help, remember?" She pursed her lips and looked me over, as if weighing my potential as a partner in crime. "Don't you worry about Saga. I'll convince him you need to come. Do not make me regret this."

I nodded, but I couldn't shake the feel that I'd be the one with the regrets.

CHAPTER 13

Bravo

I woke in a dark room. My eyes stung despite the deep shadows and my brain felt like it was trying to crack through my skull. A groan escaped my mouth before I could stop it. If one of those asshole vampires was watching me, I didn't want to give them the satisfaction of hearing my pain.

But it wasn't a vampire who answered.

"Didn't I tell you not to be a hero?"

Matri. Not happy at all.

Luckily, I was already lying on my side, because a wave of nausea rose. I angled my head over the side of the cot and threw up the potatoes I'd eaten earlier. Once my stomach was empty, I actually felt a little better. Wiping my mouth with the back of my hand, I looked up.

A scrap of damp cloth appeared in my

immediate vision, and just beyond that, Matri's stern face. Snatching the cloth with a mumbled "thanks" I made quick work of cleaning myself. When done, I pushed myself into a seated position, but instantly regretted it as the pounding behind my eyes intensified.

"Probably a concussion."

I wasn't interested in discussing my health. "You were there."

She looked away.

"You were standing there, watching, while they drained those children."

"I was." That was it. No denial. No excuses.

I spat on the floor to clear the taste of bile from my tongue. "Does that happen to all the children you *care for*?" I put mocking emphasis on the last two words.

"Yes, Bravo, it does."

Her refusal to apologize or rise to my bait enraged me. "How can you do that to them? They trust you."

She pressed her lips together and looked at me with patient pity. "They trust me to keep them alive. That is exactly what I'm doing."

"By draining them?" My raised voice ricocheted around inside my head like a bullet.

"Before I convinced the guards to use the current setup, they would snatch children from their beds and drain them dead."

My mouth fell open, but she wasn't done.

"Before I came along and convinced the camp

director that he'd have an easier time meeting his quotas with more order, this place was an all-you-can-eat buffet for the guards. A slaughterhouse." She sat on the cot next to me. I scooted as far away as I could get, still unconvinced she didn't deserve a beating for her collusion with the guards. "I know what you saw was upsetting, but I assure you it's ten times more humane than what would have occurred a few years ago."

"You expect me to thank you for that?"

"No, I expect you to work with me to make sure no children ever have to be drained again."

"What?"

She grabbed my hand and squeezed it until I stopped struggling to pull it back. "Did you wonder why I had you assigned to help me?"

I shrugged. "I gave up trying to understand your motivations around the time I saw you watching innocent children get drained."

Her hand contracted painfully on mine. "Watch yourself. You've been in this camp for a few days. I've been here for ten years. You don't know what I've seen. What I and the others have had to do to survive."

The ferocity in her tone gave me pause. I'd had to do some unsavory things, too, but if what she said about the state of life in the camp was true, then I couldn't begin to imagine what sort of terrible choices she'd had to make.

Once she saw that I got it, she continued. "When you arrived, you seemed convinced that someone was coming to save you."

I nodded. "Zed. He's coming."

"You're the first new arrival in years. Most of the rebel groups that get raided now are small groups of high bloods that band together. If they're caught, they're sent directly to the blood camps or to the Troika headquarters. We haven't had anyone with allies on the outside come in a long time."

She stopped and sighed. "I guess what I'm saying is, we haven't had a reason to hope for a long time. Not since Icarus escaped."

"Who?"

"He was one of us. A leader in the camp. He made a plan to escape, go get help, and come rescue the rest of us."

"So what happened to him?"

"He escaped all right, but he never came back for us." The pain in her voice was palpable, like acid on the ears.

We were silent for a long, heavy moment. Matri seemed lost in bitter memories, but I was busy worrying about the future. Zed would come, right? He had to.

Finally, she cleared her throat. "After Icarus left, I waited for a long time for him to come rescue us. At that point, I still had faith in him, and my goal was just to keep as many of us alive as possible until he came back. But the longer it took, the more my goal became to just stay alive, period. I knew eventually something would happen that would give us new hope. That's why I finagled my way into being in charge of the children. I figured if I could train them to be survivors then at least a few of us might be alive once hope arrived." She looked up and squeezed my hand. "And now it has."

I blew out a long, slow breath. "Look, I want nothing more than to have Zed bust down those gates and free all of us. But I have no idea how long it will take him to rally the help he'll need."

She frowned. "You mean this Zed doesn't have his own army?"

I froze. "Of course not. It was just him and me and the children."

Matri withdrew her hand and made a disgusted sound. "You're putting all your faith in your *boyfriend*?" She spat the words out like venom.

"He's not my boyfriend. He's my friend. And yes, I have every faith he will come rescue us."

She crossed her arms over her flat chest. "How can you be so sure he'll come?"

"Because we're his family," I said simply. "Besides, Zed is the most pig-headed person in history. If he decides he's going to save us, he will fight until his dying breath to make it happen."

The anger in her eyes dissipated and was replaced by a small spark. "Oh, to be young and dumb again."

"Hey!"

She patted my hand. "Sorry, dear, but it's true. It's nice you have so much faith in your friend, but it's going to take a lot more than wishes to free you from this hell."

I rose and paced away from the cot. Her words had sparked a black flame of doubt in my belly. It burned away some of the hope I'd been nurturing and left me unsure. If I didn't move, I'd cry, and I refused to give in that easily. "He'll come, and when he does, the Troika won't know what hit them."

"You said he doesn't have an army," she pointed out, her voice not as unkind as it was before.

"If I know Zed, he'll go to the Scribe."

Her brows rose. "You know Saga?"

I shook my head. "Never met him, but Zed told me lots of stories about the man in Book Mountain. If I had money, I'd bet it all on that being his first move."

Matri laughed. "And he'll find nothing. The Scribe is a myth created by the rebels. Just like that Meridian Six bitch."

I shook my head. "I don't know who that is, but I know Zed. He's coming."

She rose and sucked at the few teeth remaining in her mouth. Finally, she pursed her lips and tilted her head at me. "Then it will be up to you and me to make sure that when they arrive, the people are ready."

She came forward, spat in her palm, and held it out to me. I stared at the leathery skin for a moment, but then something happened. That black flame of doubt snuffed out and the bright light of hope exploded in my gut. I had no idea how or when Zed would arrive, but I knew that the woman standing in front of me was the right person to help me prepare for him. I spat in my palm and slapped it into hers. "Deal."

Then we sat down and began mapping out our plans.

CHAPTER 14

Meridian Six

Very little light penetrated the tiny cracks in the railcar's walls. The rhythmic sound of the train's wheels bouncing over the tracks would have been soothing had those wheels not been taking us closer to the vampire work camp with each passing second. Zed's rapid breathing and the echo of my heartbeat pounding in my own ears were the only other sounds.

The car we'd ended up inside held several crates of supplies. As promised, one of them turned up two of the blue uniforms required for all prisoners of the Krovgorod camp. On the right breast of each was embroidered the downward-pointing arrow that the Troika used to identify humans of less desirable blood types.

"How did Saga manage this?" Zed asked.

"Where Saga is concerned, I've found it's best not to ask."

He accepted this with a nod, and, for a moment, we both stared down at the uniforms that would transform us from rebels into prisoners.

According to Icarus, prisoners were issued uniforms upon their induction into the camps and would have to wear the same one for six weeks before new ones were issued. If a prisoner died from illness or injury, the head prisoner in the deceased's barracks was allowed to distribute the old uniform to anyone who needed it most. Icarus claimed people died so commonly it was rare for anyone to go the entire six weeks without a new uniform.

Zed and I donned our uniforms in silence. Once we had them on, I threw our clothes out the door of the train to remove any traces of us. The camp uniform was the cleanest and newest clothing I'd worn since I'd escaped the Troika months earlier. I'd been wearing the too-big pants, too-tight shoes, and dirty work shirt for months. I'd stolen them from Saga's junkyard after the dress the Sisters of Crimson had given me got too dirty to salvage. How long ago had it been since Sister Agrippa helped me escape into the tunnels? I'd lost track of the days and weeks since I'd escaped the Troika and landed in the rebels' clutches.

"How long until we reach the camp?" Zed

whispered.

"Not long."

I moved toward another crate, where I found two pairs of gray canvas sneakers. Mine were too big but they were a blessing after the heavy but tight boots I'd worn before. "When we get there, remember to stay hidden until the first prisoners come in to start unloading. We'll blend into the group and help unload until we can steal away to the barracks."

"What if we get split up?"

"Icarus said children under the age of twelve are all kept in a separate barracks, overseen by a few female prisoners. If we get separated, we'll meet up there."

He didn't say anything, but even in the dim light, I noted the sweat beading his brow and the shallow rise and fall of his chest. I put my hand on his shoulder. "This will work. It will. We just can't lose our nerve. If the vamps smell fear on us, we're toast."

"Won't all the humans be afraid?"

"They'll be too busy trying to hang on to life to be afraid."

He thought about this for a moment before nodding. His nostrils flared as he drew in a deep, bracing breath. "Just promise me one thing."

"Shoot."

"If anything happens to me, save Bravo and Mica. Even if you have to leave me behind."

I'd been expecting him to ask me to promise

not to leave him. Instead, he wanted me to sacrifice him to save the people he considered his family. I heard the words clearly but they didn't quite register as a concrete idea in my head. The thought of martyring myself for anyone was so foreign he might as well have made his request in Russian or Aramaic. Was there anyone alive that I'd sacrifice myself for?

Rabbit. The name popped into my head so fast I didn't have time to consciously realize I'd been the one to think it. Icarus and Dare had had my back a few times and I theirs, but if shit went down I'd save myself over them every time. But Rabbit was different. In the months since I'd joined the rebels, I'd grown to care for the scamp as if he was my own younger sibling—or child. Like the child the Troika had ripped from my belly because it had the misfortune to lose the genetic lottery and have a desirable blood type. I'm sure the psychologists who worked back before the Blood Wars would have had a field day analyzing that relationship, but I didn't give a damn. I would put myself in front of a bullet to make sure that kid had a chance at a future. He was the only one, though.

But Zed? He had protected and worried about Bravo and the children under his care for years, like a father, despite his young age. I couldn't begin to imagine the protective instincts I had for Rabbit increased by a factor of years and multiplied by seven souls.

"I told you I'd do everything in my power to avoid having to make that kind of choice on this mission."

His hand touched mine. "Meridia—"

I flinched. Hearing my Troika name—the one the rebels now used to rally humans to their cause—coming from his mouth was like a slap. I didn't want him to see me like that. Like the pawn everyone else believed me to be.

"What's wrong?" His voice was low, as if in the dim light everything took on the import of a secret.

"Can you call me Carmina?"

"Is that your real name?" he asked carefully.

I suddenly felt like the awkward one. "Meridian Six is what the vamps called me."

He paused for a moment. "Carmina it is, then."

I didn't trust myself to speak. There was something about this guy—a kindness—that I wasn't used to and wasn't sure I wanted to get too comfortable with.

"What I was going to say was whether we want to make tough choices or not, we'll have to make them. It's inevitable. I need you to promise me that you will get my family out of the camp."

"I said I would," I snapped. Just like that, the fragile bubble that had surrounded us imploded. "But you need to understand that blowing up that mine is my ticket to freedom. It has to be my priority."

His silence damned me.

"Don't you get it?" I carried on. "That's why I agreed to let you come. You focus on getting your family out and I'll focus on getting my freedom. We both win."

He smiled at me, but the expression was patronizing rather than agreeable. I suddenly felt like the worst sort of failure before the damned mission had even begun. Luckily, a hot flare of anger burned that shame off quickly. "Don't look at me like that," I said, my voice lowering to a mean register. "You don't know me or what I've been through."

"I know enough to know that you're a damned fool if you think Icarus and Saga are going to let you go if you succeed."

I crossed my arms. "What the hell does that mean?"

"It means that if you manage to blow up that mine, it will only make you a more powerful tool for the rebels. You think they're using you now? Just wait until they can parade you in front of hungry humans as the woman who took down Krovgorod."

I turned away from him. A large gap between two boards in the car's wall gave me something to stare at to avoid my discomfort. The void was filled with a blurry landscape of the Badlands—a desolate landscape of gray dirt and skeletal trees. For an instant I thought it looked a lot like how I felt inside: barren. I wanted to yell at Zed and tell him he didn't know what he was talking about. Icarus and Saga would keep their word. They had to. The alternative was unthinkable—

Cold air from the opening lashed at my face. The thin material of the prisoner's uniform did little to protect my skin from the temperature. I looked down at the ground speeding by. At my feet, which were only eighteen inches from freedom.

"Carmina." Zed's voice was quiet, as if he worried that a louder tone would startle me into action. "Don't even think about it."

It would be so easy. So simple. So final. No more scratching out a pitiful existence, and for what? In the vain hope that one day I'd know the sweet flavor of freedom? I'd been so young when the vampires enslaved us that I couldn't say I even knew what it tasted like. I imagined it tasted a lot like grapefruits—like sunshine and sweetness. But I was lying to myself, wasn't I? Because if I were being honest, I'd also admit that there was plenty of sour too.

Freedom meant I couldn't blame anyone else for how shitty my life was. It meant I had to make my own decisions. God, I was so tired.

"Carmina." A warm hand touched my arm. A single spot of heat in a world gone totally cold. "Come here."

I looked away from the blur of gray to the face of this boy I barely knew but was now bound to for survival.

"We can do this," he said. His hand squeezed my arm. The touch felt real, more real than the nightmare out there—the desolation, the gray, the dead-end world. "We can and we will."

I turned my head to look out the door again, but his hand grabbed my chin, refusing to let me be wooed by the promise of nothingness. He turned my chin, forcing me to look at him. "You have more power than you know."

I jerked back out of his grasp. "You don't know me."

"I know that you use tough words to hide your fear. I know that you want nothing to do with fighting. I know that you fight anyway because it's not in your nature to surrender."

I looked away, my cheeks heating with shame.

"You wouldn't have done it," he said.

"How do you know?" I asked, looking at my feet.

"Because you could have killed yourself a thousand times while you were in the hands of the Troika. And since then, you know damned well no one could stop you if it's what you really wanted." He let those words sink in for a few moments. "But I also know that even if I'm right about Saga and Icarus, you will still find a way to claim the freedom you want so badly."

I laughed, but the sound had no humor to it. "Oh yeah? How will I manage that?"

He shrugged. "Only one way to find out—unless you're too scared to try."

I'd only known Zed for a couple of days, but already he'd figured out the best way to motivate me. I hated him for that as much as I appreciated the kick in the ass. No matter what happened once we reached the camp, I wouldn't let anyone tell me how to live anymore. I just had to survive long enough to be able to flip everyone the bird before I walked away.

CHAPTER 15

Bravo

The train arrived at sunrise two days later.

I'd just started getting used to the reverse sleeping schedule, so when Matri shook me awake just after dawn, I had trouble reaching full consciousness.

"Rise and shine," she whispered. "We have to take some of the children and go unload the train."

The train meant meat, clean uniforms, and other rations. It was daytime, so our work unloading the cars would be overseen by some of the human guards, who I'd discovered were more sadistic than the vampires.

Since my talk with Matri, we'd been busy studying ways that we could make an escape possible. This involved stockpiling some supplies under the floorboards of the barracks and informing the other prisoners that they needed to be on the lookout for signs a breakout was imminent. The only problem was I had no idea what form those signs would come in—or when.

Beyond that, I'd spent most of the previous two days keeping an eye on Mica. Matri had made sure he hadn't been drained of too much blood for his first bleeding, and also got him extra rations to restore his strength quickly. Granted, those extra rations were just extra potatoes, but it was better than what most of the prisoners had.

The human guard Matri called Judas stood outside the barracks with two other guards to lead us to the warehouse next to the train track. It wasn't a long walk to the depot, but the guards took us through a part of camp I'd yet to see. The entrance to the mines was located in the northernmost quadrant. We passed nearby, and for the first time I saw the yawning black hole that swallowed most of the camp's workers every night and day. Even though most of the activity in the camp happened at night, the miners dug and scraped and hauled twenty-four hours a day.

As we passed, a train that looked vaguely like a centipede was chugging toward the hole. Workers, their skin perpetually blackened from coal dust, packed the seats and stared grimly into the mine, which gaped like an empty eye socket.

The previous shift emerged from the hole in a single-file line. Their hair, their skin, and their uniforms—all black. Only their eyes, painfully white, gave any relief to the all-black canvas.

My steps faltered as I gawped, but I quickly received the stab of a gun muzzle to my back as a reminder to keep moving. Honestly, I was relieved to leave them behind. Those artificially bright orbs set in pitch-black faces would haunt my dreams. Even if they got free from the camp, there's no way they'd live long enough to enjoy their freedom. They were the walking dead.

Soon enough, we reached the warehouse that was set on a raised platform next to the train tracks. The last time I'd been there was the day we arrived at the camp in cattle cars. This train wasn't here to deliver people, but supplies, so they were all solid metal shipping cars.

A handful of humans whose camp jobs fell under more administrative labor were standing on the platform with clipboards bearing shipping manifests. They directed the workflow for us and all the other prisoners who had been recruited to unload the train. Matri took a small group of children toward the livestock car to begin the process of counting heads of pigs and chickens. Meanwhile, I was instructed to take my group of children toward a car filled with uniforms. We were to count the boxes inside and report them to the administrators before delivering the uniforms to the warehouse for storage.

The door to our car was already cracked open. I thought nothing of this as I pushed it open and shooed the children inside, eager to get started. I'd spent the previous day helping the youngs pick potatoes, and the change of pace appealed to me.

I'd taken two steps inside when a high gasp sounded from one of the children. Before I could locate the source of the sound, an arm wrapped around my throat. Then a woman's voice—low and mean—hissed in my ear. "Do not scream."

I swallowed against the knot of fear in my throat but managed to nod.

"Good. Now tell the brats to calm the fuck down. We're not going to hurt you unless the guards come running."

I looked across the way to where the three children I'd brought into the car huddled together, whimpering. I held a finger to my lips. Meanwhile, my brain was spinning, trying to catch up. If this person was worried about the guards coming then she wasn't a friend of the Troika's. But was she an ally?

"I'm Bravo," I said.

A shadow moved to my right. A male shape emerged from behind two crates. A shaft of light cut through the open doors and caught his face.

I nearly collapsed in relief, but the damned arm against my windpipe tightened. "Not so fast."

"Six," Zed hissed. "It's her—this is Bravo."

The arm suddenly disappeared and I stumbled. Zed's arms crushed me to him. I didn't fall apart. No sobs broke free from my chest. But I grabbed onto him so hard that he finally whispered in an amused tone, "You're hurting me."

I pulled back a few inches to see that his eyes were shiny with tears. "Pussy," I said.

He chuckled and pulled me in for another hug. "I'm so glad you're alive." He pushed me back again to look at my face. "Mica?"

I bit my lip. It was too soon to tell him about the bleeding, but technically the young was okay as could be, given the situation. "He's okay. We've been taken in by a woman who oversees the child laborers." My stomach twisted with excitement and fear. Excitement because I never would have imagined Zed would come so fast, but fear because his arrival meant things had just gotten way more dangerous for everyone. "I told her you'd come." I grabbed his shoulders and squeezed. "I knew you'd come for us."

The corner of his mouth lifted in a wobbly sideways grin. "I'm sorry it took so long. I was worried you'd already broken out."

An annoyed-sounding throat cleared behind us. "If the touching reunion is over, we've got work to do."

I turned to look at the woman who'd had me in a headlock. From the physical assault and the bitchiness, I figured she'd be six feet tall and ugly. Turns out I was half right. She was barely taller than me—probably five-eight, but she looked like someone had beaten her with the ugly stick. Pale scalp peeked out between the dark stubble on her head. Her right eye was swollen almost totally shut. The other one had fared only slightly better, in that it was swollen but a bloodshot pupil was clearly visible. Her lip was split and her jaw was covered in purple bruises. The wounds distorted her face too much to tell what she'd looked like before she lost the fight.

"Who the hell are you?" I asked.

She snorted. "I'm Carmina."

Zed stiffened next to me, and I looked up at him to see what was wrong. He gave the female a look I couldn't read. She just cocked her head at him, as if in challenge. Finally, she looked at me. "And you're Bravo."

I nodded toward her swollen face. "Who beat your ass?"

"Someone a lot tougher than you, little girl."

"All right," Zed said. "I swear, if you both had dicks you'd be measuring them."

I didn't like this Carmina. I knew this was not a rational reaction to have about someone who had come to help save my ass, so I decided to push down my hostility. "Sorry, it's been a shitty week," I said.

Her lips quirked into a smile, as if I'd surprised her. And just like that, the tension dissipated. "How many guards?" She nodded toward the door.

"Three. Humans. All have rifles."

She nodded. "We'll wait until the unloading gets under way and blend into the crowd."

CHAPTER 16

Meridian Six

An hour later, we entered Matri's domain. Sneaking off the train was easier than I'd expected, but the human guards who made up the Troika's day shift were lazy fools. They leaned against the train depot like slugs, smoking cigarettes and gossiping like old ladies. Bravo had led us and the children into the warehouse to deliver the boxes of uniforms before leading us right out the back door.

We'd met Matri on the path to the barracks. She'd given each of us a once-over with her miss-nothing gaze and nodded. "All right," she said. "All right."

Then she'd lowered her head to listen to one of the children. She'd listened to the girl as if the young was an oracle delivering our fates when in fact she'd only been asking Matri when they'd have their next meal. "Soon, sugar. Soon." Then she'd run her hand over the child's greasy hair and smiled like they were in a park on a picnic instead of walking through a death camp.

Sure, Icarus had told me that Krovgorod was a labor camp. He'd explained how the mining operation worked and how the rest of the prisoners each had shifts in different sections of the camp, but being there put the entire operation in a different light. For one thing, the people were walking corpses. So thin. And their skin was either gray from the constant plume of ashes from the main warehouse's furnaces or pitch black from the coalmines.

The barracks she led us to wasn't much larger than the train car we'd so recently abandoned. The wooden structure was filled with rows of rough-hewn bunk beds. The air stank of body odor and urine. There was no light. No hope. It was little better than a tomb. Stepping inside, I looked at Zed, who'd gone pale. He shot a look at Bravo, who tried to smile, but it came out wobbly, as if she was ashamed for us to see how they'd been living.

But instead of pity, I felt anger. Icarus had warned me the conditions would be bad— subhuman. But nothing prepared me to see thirty-odd children living like livestock in a wooden pen. Their dirty faces had long forgotten how to smile and as they watched us enter, their faces were blank, as if they'd also forgotten how to hope.

"I've sent a couple of the children to round up the camp leaders."

I walked to a long wooden table near the front of the room. My fingers itched for a gun. The minute I'd walked into that room I'd lost the illusion of being a tourist in the camp. The instant Zed and I had revealed ourselves, we'd committed to being prisoners too. I just hoped it was a temporary situation rather than a permanent one.

Zed didn't join me at the table. Instead, he joined Bravo and a small boy. He knelt down so the kid, who couldn't have been older than ten, could squeeze his arms around Zed's neck. As the boy reached for him, I spotted wounds on the inside of his elbow. Perfect little puncture marks like a needle—or fangs—would make.

The sight made my stomach cramp with disgust. The guards didn't waste their time helping themselves to the fresh blood.

Matri saw me staring and sidled closer. "What's your name?

I glanced at her, surprised she didn't recognize me, but then I remembered the state of my face. "Carmina."

Her eyes widened. "Carmina Sargosa?" she whispered, looking around to be sure no one else heard.

I froze. "You've heard that name?" Most of

the humans I'd run into had heard of Meridian Six because of the Troika's propaganda campaign. Carmina Sargosa—the name my mother had given me—was a name even the rebels refused to use because they believed it lacked the power of my Troika-given name.

Matri nodded. "I've seen your face every day for the last decade." A rueful look crept over her face. "Although I wouldn't have recognized you looking like this."

I touched the bruises on my cheek. "We were afraid the guards would recognize me."

She nodded. "Smart. You two got a plan?"

Her segue was so abrupt it took me a moment to respond. "Blow shit up and run."

She laughed out loud. "No, really."

I stared at her long enough for it to sink in that I wasn't joking.

"Where are your bombs, then, girl?"

"The mines. Someone has to know where the dynamite is kept."

Matri snorted. "We all know where they are. You think we don't? The problem is getting past the bats and the guards."

"Look, I got a train and a plan to blow up the mines. You got a better plan, I'd like to hear it."

She crossed her arms. "Thought you'd come with more."

"Lady, do you have any idea the risk we took just sneaking the two of us inside?"

"I do," she said. "I just hope it's enough.

Because if we don't figure out how to get out of here by sundown, you're going to be joining our little resort permanently."

I frowned. "Why sundown?"

"When the vampires emerge from their underground bunkers at sundown, the first thing they do is take a roll call of all the prisoners."

Cold sweat broke out on my back. Icarus hadn't mentioned that detail. "Shit."

"You got that right, girlie." She started to say something else, but at that moment, three other people walked in the door. A very tall man of Asian origin entered first. The woman was unremarkable except for the bright red skin of her hands. The second man worked in the mines, which I knew instantly from the artificial blackness of his skin.

"Ah, here they are," Matri said, moving to greet them. "This is Wu."

The Asian guy came forward. "My name is Alex. Everyone here just calls me Wu because they're ignorant."

I ignored the jab at his fellow prisoners. "Nice to meet you, Alex."

Matri snorted, as if she thought he was joking, but it was clear from his expression he was not. "Anyway, this is Cleo, she runs the wash house, where they clean the guard's uniforms." I nodded to the woman with red hands as Matri turned to the final man. "And this is Tuck, he obviously works the mines."

He tipped down his chin, but made no other move to greet me. It was hard not to stare at his black skin and white eyes, so I forced my gaze to return to Matri.

"This is Carmina Sargosa. You may have heard her called Meridian Six."

My stomach dipped. I'd hoped to keep my real identity a secret. If any of the guards caught us and found out who I really was, this was going to go from dangerous to downright suicidal. "Actually, it's probably best if we all avoid mentioning that."

Before Matri could respond, Alex spoke. "The Troika's whore? What the hell is she doing here, Matri? She's a spy."

"No," I said, "I'm not. I escaped the Troika months ago and went underground. I've been working for the rebels ever since." There was no point asking if any of them had heard about the attack on the factory. I was pretty sure the Troika would do everything in their power to keep the prisoners from hearing any news from the outside—especially when it involved embarrassment for the vampires.

"She's telling the truth," Zed said, coming over to join us. "After Bravo and the youngs were taken by a Troika patrol, I went to Saga."

Murmurs spread through the room. Clearly the Scribe's reputation was well known.

"He's the one who asked Carmina to help me infiltrate the prison."

Alex looked skeptical. "How many are in your army? Are they outside the walls?"

Zed's face fell. "You don't understand. There is no army. It's just us."

Silence descended over the barracks. Alex, Cleo, and Tuck all looked to Matri as if wanting her to confirm Zed was joking. She just shrugged.

"Look," I said, "we may not have an army, but we do have a plan."

Tuck sighed. "Make it fast. I'm due on shift in half an hour."

"We need to create a diversion. There's dynamite in the camp somewhere, right? You have to use it for mining."

"Don't be crazy. The vamps would never let any of us near it. They use the human guards to do the blasting if it's needed during the day."

"So we'll just have to convince one of the humans to give us the key."

He shook his head. "With what weapons, girl? With what strength? We're all half-starved."

"We'll use their weapons."

Tuck waved a dismissive hand in my direction, but he didn't speak to me. Instead, he tuned to Matri. "This is a waste of time."

"We're the only chance you got," I said. "You think anyone else is coming for you?"

He stopped and looked at me. "Let's say you get the dynamite. Then what? The front gates are locked fifteen ways to Sunday. Only open with permission from the camp director."

"That gate won't stand up against a train going full speed."

He didn't sound as impressed as I'd hoped. Instead he walked toward me. He looked like a living shadow of a man. "Tell me this, smart girl, how you gonna decide who stays and who goes?"

CHAPTER 17

Matri

The girl had spunk. You had to give her that. Unlike Bravo, who worked very hard to appear confident, Six wore her bravery like a comfortable second skin. But brave ain't the same as smart.

"I said, how are you going to decide who stays or who goes?" Tuck repeated. "That train can only hold a couple hundred people. This camp has thousands of prisoners."

Carmina remained silent, but her skin paled. Her eyes took on a hunted look, as if she hadn't considered liberating the entire camp.

Like I said, brave ain't the same as smart.

"Did you really expect us all to help you save yourselves while the rest of us stay behind?" I snorted. "You put all of us in danger just by being here. If the Troika catch you, we'll all be punished."

Behind me, worried chatter and panic rose on the air. I held up a hand. The chatter lessened but the panic was still palpable.

"We'll take as many as we can," Zed said.

The girl didn't look in his direction. She was watching me, trying to decide if she could win me to her cause or if I was just another obstacle in her way.

"It does no one any good to take risks that doom all of us," she said finally. "Trying to free everyone will be impossible. When we fail, the Troika will kill all of us."

I crossed my arms. "Why shouldn't we just kill you right now?"

Zed stepped forward, his shoulders back and his hands curled into fists. That one was a fighter. Too bad he wouldn't live long enough to prove it.

"Killing us only guarantees you'll all die in this camp."

"I already made peace with that, girl."

"If we can get out of here alive, we'll be able to make a plan for a more focused attack. Raise enough of an army to make a real liberation attempt."

"An army?" I laughed. "Sweetheart, the workers in this camp outnumber the vampires fifty to one. We have superior numbers, but they have the weapons, the power, and every other advantage over us. It's not an army we need. It's a miracle."

Six threw up her hands. "So you're going to lie down and die? You've given up? Fine. That's your choice. I'm leaving with those children tonight. If you want to help, fine. We'll take everyone out of here that we can. But you're never going to convince me that it's better to surrender than to try, damn it."

The room fell silent. The pressure of dozens of expectant stares weighed against my skin.

"There might be a way to save the rest of the prisoners," Tuck said.

I glanced at him in surprise.

He smiled. "The minute y'all take that train, the guards are gonna swarm you like angry wasps."

"Yeah, so?" I said.

"So the distraction might give the rest of us time to hide in the mines. There's water and air shafts down there. Could probably survive a couple of days if y'all come back to help us."

The room fell silent as this sunk in.

Finally, Zed said, "That might work. You'll be protected from the explosions and we can come back to dig you out once the vamps are cooked."

"This is a pipe dream," I said. "You'll die in those mines and the rest of you will die trying to make a break for it." I shook my head. "I used to have hope too." I sighed to release the pressure of disappointment in my chest. "I had it back when I was young and thought that life would work out for me if I only wanted it badly enough.

But then I grew up and realized that those stories of heroism we were raised on were just fictions created to fool us into believing life is worth the trouble."

"If you really think that, why are you still here?"

"You mean, why haven't I killed myself?"

Six nodded.

"Because I'm too stubborn to prove them right."

"Who?"

I nodded toward the door. "The vampires. They want us to believe that we don't matter. If I give up the only things I have left—the air in my lungs, the blood in my veins—then I'm only proving them right."

Zed stepped into the conversation, forming the third point of a triangle. "Then help us."

"What's in it for me?"

Six raised her chin. "They crave our surrender. They want us to give up our blood, our lives, our hope. I say we show them that humanity still has some fight left in it. If we're going to die anyway, let it happen with our feet on the ground and our fists flying."

Behind Six, Cleo was rubbing her red hands together. Tuck's white teeth flashed as he chewed contemplatively on his lower lip. Only Wu looked unmoved by the girl's passionate speech. His expression was as skeptical as it had been from the minute the conversation started.

I raised an eyebrow and watched Cleo for a reaction. When it came, the nod was almost too subtle to see, but then she glanced at Tuck, whose lips spread to reveal aggressively bright teeth, gleaming like stars against a night sky.

Something tugged at the hem of my tunic. Little Finn looked up at me. He was only as tall as my waist and barely wider than one of the floor planks. "Matri," he said, "are we really going to leave?"

The backs of my eyeballs stung and my chest tightened painfully. This was crazy. I wasn't ready for this. I'd spent the last several years in survival mode. Trying to do whatever it took to keep the children alive and curry favor with the vampires and the traitors to buy us some time. But now I realized I'd been buying time for this. Buying time for something—or someone—to come along and give us a reason to hope again.

I placed a hand on little Finn's head and smiled at him even though emotion was making my lips tremble. "We're done here."

Whether we were leaving the camp for the outside world or leaving our mortal bodies, I didn't know. I just finally understood that taking this risk was better than extending the dead-end lives we'd all been living.

I looked at Meridian Six, whose own eyes were red, as if she'd been dealing with a sting of her own. "All right," I said. "What's the plan?"

CHAPTER 18

Zed

The sun was too low. After we'd convinced Matri and the others to help, we'd wasted too much time trying to adjust the original plan. It had been a necessary step, but every minute that passed took us closer and closer to the hour of doom, when the monsters crawled out of their bunkers.

After we'd made the plan, Six told me to work with Tuck on getting enough dynamite and slipped out the door. My decision to ignore her order took about two seconds. I chased her outside and stopped her before she could march off.

"I told you to talk to Tuck." She jerked her arm out of my hand.

"Where are you going?"

"I have my own mission." Her posture was stiff, as if she was bracing for a physical fight instead of just an argument.

"You're going after Dr. Death?"

She met my eyes but didn't speak.

"You can't go alone."

"Wrong. I *have* to go alone."

"No you don't. You don't have to kill him at all. Let's get the train loaded up and get the hell out of here before the vamps wake up."

She placed a hand on my cheek. Her palm was calloused, but I found myself pressing into her touch because it had been so long since anyone had touched me with any sort of comfort. "You save your kids. Don't worry about me."

I jerked my head away from her touch. The patronizing edge to her tone pissed me off. "If you want to commit suicide, it's your choice, but don't act like you're some sort of martyr here."

She had the nerve to look wounded. "I-I'm not a martyr."

"Bullshit. You know that's exactly what Saga and Icarus want, don't you? A glorious memory they can hold up to all the rebels to inspire them. Poor Meridian Six who died for the cause just like her mother."

Pain exploded across my cheek before I realized she'd slapped me. The throbbing eased just as she spun and marched off toward the center of camp. "Six!" I repeated her name two more times. On the second try, she threw her middle finger up over her head and picked up speed.

I sighed and rubbed at my hot cheek. What the hell was I supposed to do now? My legs itched like maybe I should chase her, but my pride reminded me that if I chased her it would be like admitting I was wrong. I was not wrong. She knew that, which was why she'd hit me.

Bravo was in charge of rounding up the children, and I needed to go help Tuck with the explosives. Instead, I stood in the dusty air and watched Six's retreat. Something deep in my center—not my heart, but my gut—told me that if I let her walk away I'd never see her again.

"Damn it." I hissed the words aloud, almost as if to give myself a chance to change my mind. But I didn't. I took off in a jog that quickly turned in to a run. Tuck could get the dynamite without my help, but I wasn't about to let Six murder that vampire alone.

———

When I caught up with her, she'd reached a part of the camp I hadn't yet seen. It was a central square of sorts. If it had been the center of a town back before the war, it would have had a courthouse with a small diner across the street. But this was a prison camp, so the center of the dusty square was dominated by a flagpole bearing the Troika's black flag and red lightning symbol. On each of the four sides, a different building stood. One was obviously the barracks for the guards, which looked like a luxury condo block compared to the shacks the prisoners were forced to live in. Another building was most likely the mess hall and another was a laundry used specifically for the vampires. I'd seen the meager prisoner washhouse, which was made up of little more than tin wash bins with cakes of lye soap. This place, however, looked like it held a variety of modern industrial washers and dryers, along with pressing machines to ensure the guards had knife-pleats in their pants while they beat the prisoners.

I reached Six when she was almost at the flagpole. Before she saw me, she'd already paused and was staring off in the fourth direction, which I had yet to observe in my rush to reach her. I paused beside her. She didn't look at me, but I felt sure she knew I was there. I didn't want to speak first, so I followed her gaze.

The fourth edge of the square held a large cinderblock palace. The Troika's symbol was on display at the top of the building, like a marquee, but that wasn't what had captured her attention.

A massive banner hung over the building's door. On it, Meridian Six looked up toward the sky, as if looking to the future. Her hair was tied back into a bun and she wore the gray uniform of a high-ranking human slave—the kind that was trained in the special "education" centers in Nachtstadt. The slogan underneath the image said, *Freedom through blood. Life through labor.*

That's when the shame hit me. I pulled my gaze from the image to look at her face. The sharp contrast between the clear, unblemished skin of the beauty on the banner versus the swollen and bruised face of the woman next to me was painful. I'd just told her that she was being used, as if it was something that might never have occurred to her. But now I understood that being used was all she'd ever known.

"I'm sorry," I whispered.

"You were right." She didn't look at me.

"I know. I'm still sorry."

She tipped her chin. I wasn't sure if she was accepting my apology or simply acknowledging that she'd heard me. Either way, I didn't feel better.

"I have to kill him." She said it simply, like stating a fact, such as "I need oxygen to live."

"Why?"

She turned to look at me then. Her eyes shone like new nickels. "I was…shared with him."

Suddenly I needed to kill him too.

"Let's go." I started to walk toward the building with its banner that displayed Six like some sort of blood trophy.

She grabbed my arm. "Wait. Don't you have to help Tuck—"

I jerked my hand out of her grasp and stepped toward her, getting close enough to whisper. "We are all getting out of here. All of us. Got it?"

She looked taken aback, as if she hadn't suspected I was capable of anger. I wished I could tell her exactly how I was feeling. About how the idea of her being passed around by the bloodsuckers made me want to burn the entire world down. About how I wanted to grab her and hold her until she believed that there were people in the world who didn't see her as a thing to be used. About how I wanted to tell her that I wasn't just a kid for her to patronize. But I also knew that she'd laugh and reject all of those thoughts. Instead, I'd have to show her what I meant. How I felt.

She watched me with an unreadable expression for a few tense moments. I braced myself for the arguments I knew she was formulating. But she surprised me.

"Suit yourself, but when the time comes, I get the kill on Dr. Death. Understand?"

I didn't understand why she needed to be the one, but I didn't argue. "Let's go."

CHAPTER 19

Meridian Six

The good thing about having vampires as an enemy was that they loved tunnels. Whenever the Troika took over a new city or town, the first thing they always did was turn the Earth under that town into an underground maze—like a rabbit warren. In fact, the first time I met Dare and Icarus was in a set of tunnels under the Sisters of Blood convent. The abandoned tunnels had been used during the Blood Wars and after the vamps had taken over New York and turned it into their capital, Nachtstadt, to escape the Troika's slaughter patrols.

The tunnels under the blood camps were still in use; they were clean and well lit. According to Matri, the vamps use them to transport laundry and food to the main building, where the top officers lived and worked. Special prisoners were given access since they provided the labor for those services. Prisoners who'd earned the honor wore special red uniforms. The vampire in charge of the uniforms was a female guard called Billy. I didn't know her real name, nor did I care, but Matri told me the nickname referred to the female's resemblance to a goat. "She's about as smart as one too," Matri had added.

The thing I learned about vampires—especially those on power trips, and weren't they all?—was that they always underestimated humans. If they'd respected us as foes or recognized that our desperation made us determined and resourceful, they would have assigned more guards. But as it happened, Billy was alone.

She rose from her chair—and rose and rose. Matri hadn't mentioned that Billy was well over six feet tall. Her eyes were wide apart, almost on the sides of her face instead of anywhere near the center. Her pupils weren't vertical like a goat's but her irises were pure black and lacking all empathy.

The uniform vault was located inside a caged room. Through the door behind Billy, I could see rows of different-colored uniforms on racks that rose several feet in the air. The plain uniforms we'd brought with us on the train that day filled most of the room, but my eye was drawn to a single row of red uniforms on the top bar. It wouldn't be easy to reach them, but first we had to get through Billy.

"You're not allowed in here." Her voice was scratchy and high, but paired with her imposing size the effect was unsettling. "Who sent you?"

Zed bowed his head and whispered, "Matri sent us."

Billy frowned. "She has no authority here. Go." She crossed her arms to punctuate the command.

"She said we were to report here to get uniforms." He stepped forward to continue speaking, but his hands were behind his back and he waved his fingers to the right.

I glanced that direction. Strapped to the wall was a long pole with a hook on the end. I realized this must be the tool Billy used to reach the uniforms on the upper racks. The hook had a protrusion at the top. It wasn't sharp enough to cut through flesh on its own, but with enough weight I might be able to break skin.

Billy came around to the front of the metal desk. "Leave or I will have you taken to the Komandant's office."

As it happened, that's exactly where we wanted to be, but not that way. "I'm sure this is just a misunderstanding," I said. "We've only just arrived to the camp and were assigned to the children's barracks. Matri said she didn't have enough uni—"

"I do not care. This is not how things are done." She was already reaching for the phone.

"Wait!" Zed said, leaping forward.

Billy sprung around with a hiss and flashed a large set of fangs. Zed froze, his hands raised to show he meant no harm.

"Do not move." Her voice was low and mean, filled with deadly promise. She turned back around to grab the phone.

I grabbed the pole off the wall and swung it around. Zed ducked just as the hook sliced the air above his head. I ran and pushed all my weight behind the pole and thrust it toward Billy's back.

Just as the tip made contact, she turned. The point bounced off her shoulder blade and glanced across the broad plane of her back. Because of the length of the pole, I didn't have the luxury of turning quickly. Spinning back around took forever, and by the time I managed it, Billy was ready for me.

She came at me with a snarl of fangs and fists.

"Carmina!" Zed yelled.

From the corner of my eye, I saw a flash of movement as he moved to help, but I was too preoccupied with the knuckles slamming into my cheekbone to feel relief. The pole fell from my fingers as I stumbled back.

Vampires are stronger and faster than any human. They live incredibly long lives as long as they get enough blood to heal their wounds, but they are not immortal. I had to remain calm enough to wait for my opening and quick enough to stay alive.

Billy swung again, but this time I was ready for her and ducked. Air swished by my face. She grunted as Zed attacked her from behind. His distraction gave me enough time to grab the pole again. The wood cracked over my knee, which made the pole a much more manageable length for close-quarters combat.

By the time I stood upright again, Billy was tossing Zed like a sack of laundry. I swung the pole around my head and cracked it across the side of her face. Her head spun and a fan of blood flew across the desk. She stumbled to the side as her hand went to her broken jaw. I spun around again to increase my momentum and this time, thrust the tip of the hook straight up under her chin. The soft skin gave easily and the pole slid home inside her skull with a sickening crunch.

Her black eyes widened and a wet gurgle came out of her bloody mouth. When gravity took over, it was like watching a tree fall.

My hands were shaking. I told myself it was because I'd been gripping my makeshift weapon so hard, but that didn't explain the nausea or the creeping sense that things were going to get a whole lot worse before the day was done.

Ignoring the adrenaline hangover, I went to help Zed up. When he rose, he winced and favored his right leg.

"Is it broken?" I asked in a clipped tone. I didn't have time to play nursemaid. We'd made a lot of racket killing Billy, and if we didn't get moving we'd lose our window.

"Twisted," he said. "It's fine." But when he took an experimental step, he hissed. "Shit."

"Hold on." I ran to Billy's body and removed the keys that were clipped to her waist. As I opened the cage, my mind was scrambling to form a new plan. There was no way Zed could limp into the main building. Not only was it impractical but it would also destroy our ruse that we were favored workers. Vampires would never allow an injured human to take on such an important responsibility. They would be too disgusted by the display of human frailty to allow it in the main building.

Inside the cage, I realized my other problem. Not only had I broken the pole that had been used to reach the special uniforms, but what was left of it was currently impaled in Billy's skull.

Looking up, I realized that if I stood on my tiptoes, I could just reach the hem of the closest red uniform. I looked around for something to use. Billy's chair lay on its side just beyond the door. I ran over and pulled it into the cage. After that, it was a simple matter to get what I needed.

"You only got one," Zed said. There was accusation in his tone and his eyes were bright, like he was ready to fight. I realized he thought I planned on leaving him there.

I shook my head. "Change of plans."

"We discussed this—"

"Stop," I interrupted. I grabbed the laundry cart that sat just inside the cage and pushed it out. "Get in."

He paused and his eyes went from angry to surprised. "I'll be damned."

I smiled. "I'll cover you with extra uniforms." I flicked a glanced toward the dead vampire. "But first we need to hide her."

———

Ten minutes later, we locked the cage behind us. Inside, another laundry cart held my old clothes and Billy's body. If we were lucky, no one would come along looking for her before we were on the train.

The fabric of the red uniforms was finer than the rough, beige material of the old one, but it felt itchy and constricting. "You okay?" I said in an undertone to the cart.

From deep within piles of fabric, a muffled "okay" emerged. Buried with Zed was a gun we'd found in Billy's desk as well as a knife. I'd have felt a lot better with one of them against my skin, but we couldn't risk a guard patting me down on my way into the main building. As it was, we were praying none of them thought to search the cart.

I knew from Matri's instructions that Dr. Death's lab was located in the fourth subbasement of the main building. His personal apartments were connected to the lab rooms, and could only be accessed through a heavily guarded corridor. Because of his exalted position within the camp and the Troika, no humans were allowed to serve him. He had his own staff of servants that saw to all of his personal needs.

However, humans were allowed to collect his laundry. All of his garments were sent up to the main level via a mechanized chute. The items were collected by prisoners who then transported them to the laundry facilities, where they were washed in separate machines by a squad of vampire workers.

The sun was still up, but not for long. If we could kill Dr. Death and get out of the building before the sun was down we'd stand a better chance of making it to the station. The sun wouldn't kill them, but ultra-violet light wreaked havoc on their immune systems and weakened them substantially. That's why they relied on human guards to patrol during the day. If the human prisoners rose up together against sun-weakened vampire guards they'd stand a much better chance of winning than they would have at night.

I made it through the tunnel and pushed the cart into the first basement level of the main building. A vampire guard stood just inside, but waved us through without a word. I'd worried a guard might think it was odd for us to bring dirty clothes into the building, but clearly this one was too bored to care about anything.

A freight elevator stood about twenty feet beyond where I entered. I walked slowly so as not to attract too much attention, but not slow enough to earn me a reprimand for being lazy. As I walked, I spotted other workers bustling around to prepare for the evening meal and the night's activities. A couple cast looks in my direction that made me wonder if they were in on what was about to happen.

The elevator opened and I pushed the cart inside. As the doors closed, a starburst of fear popped in my stomach. If one of the prisoners decided to try to curry favor with the vamps, they could easily blow the whistle on our plan. Images of Dr. Death lying in wait several floors below my feet paraded through my mind's eye.

The rub was there would be no way of knowing if there would be an ambush until it was too late. At that point, I had no choice but to move forward and deliver myself into fate's hands. I just hoped Zed had that gun ready to go when we got off the elevator. I didn't dare speak to him to confirm that, though, because I knew I was being watched by some faceless vampire in a control room somewhere in the building. That was also why I needed to act fast once we got into Dr. Death's lab. The minute shit started going down, there'd be a phalanx of guards deployed to take us out.

The elevator stopped on the right floor. I sucked in a deep breath. The floor indicator dinged. I exhaled and white-knuckled the cart as the doors opened.

But instead of seeing a squad of death dealers on the other side, an empty hallway greeted us. My heart didn't stop galloping until I pushed the cart into the hallway and realized we really were alone. By the looks of it, this level was filled with storerooms. No living quarters or offices in sight.

Under my breath, I whispered, "We're alone, but be ready."

A whisper of sound emerged from the pile of uniforms.

I moved down the hall as quickly as I could without calling too much attention to myself if anyone was watching. At the end of that hall, there was a turn, and halfway down the next hall a metal door was cut into the wall. Each floor had a door to the dumbwaiter, so clothing, food, or supplies could easily be delivered directly to Dr. Death from almost any floor in the building without him needing to leave his rooms.

I looked around for any telltale red lights that might indicate a camera hidden in any of the vents or nooks in the hallway but didn't see any. I knew better than to trust that thought so I took a moment to collect myself before I got started.

I opened the door and cursed. Inside, the space was barely large enough for a child. Even Rabbit would have had a hard time squeezing into the cube. "Shit," I whispered.

The uniforms moved until there was a hole just large enough for Zed to speak through. "What's wrong?"

"Change of plans." While he lifted his head just enough to see the problem, I got busy pushing buttons to send the dumbwaiter up a floor. "We're going to have to climb down the chute."

By that point, anyone watching would have already deployed guards, but there were no sirens or alarms echoing through the building. It was possible they wouldn't raise a general alarm, but just send guards to dispose of us quietly and quickly. Either way, we needed to get moving.

"You go first," I said. "Take the gun but give me the knife."

He climbed out of the cart and glanced down into the chute. "Six, it's a sheer drop to the next floor. I'll break a leg."

We didn't have time to argue, so I just started grabbing uniforms and tying the legs together to create a makeshift rope. He instantly caught on and pitched in without arguing. I had to admit working with Zed was a pleasant change from being with Icarus and Dare, who questioned everything I did—loudly. With both of us working, it only took a couple of minutes to create a long enough rope to lower Zed down.

"What are you going to do once I'm down?" he asked.

"I'll tie it to the handle. Even if it breaks as I go down, it'll reduce the length of my fall."

He didn't look happy about my solution, but he was smart enough to know there was no other choice. "Let's go."

He grabbed one end of the rope and waited until I'd put the other end around my waist as a counterweight. Without another word, he began rappelling down the long, metal throat. I braced one leg against the wall and leaned back against the pull of the rough fabric loop around my waist. Once he was down, I needed to be ready to move quickly or he'd be trapped down there alone with Dr. Death. There wasn't a place to land and wait for me, so he'd basically have to climb out the door and into the rooms below before I could begin my descent.

It took less time than I expected for him to reach the spot two floors below. Before I was ready, he pushed off the wall and kicked open the door into Dr. Death's inner sanctum. "Now, Six!"

I fumbled for a moment with the rope but quickly tied it to the door handle. I stuck the knife he'd given me in the waistband of my uniform. I was just swinging my feet over the edge of the hole when shouts sounded below.

As I leaped into the chute, a gunshot exploded below me.

CHAPTER 20

Zed

Behind me, crashing sounds and feminine grunts signaled my partner's arrival. I didn't dare look that direction because I was too busy aiming my gun at the servant I'd stumbled into when I came out of the chute. He wore simple gray clothes of a finer cloth than the prisoners I'd seen, which made sense seeing how he worked for the head of the camp. His head was bald and his lips were disconcertingly red, as if he'd recently fed and had forgotten to wipe them with a napkin.

I'd fired a warning shot when he'd refused to stop coming toward me. Luckily, the bullet that flew past his head and lodged into the wall behind him convinced him to stay put, but now we faced one another across the bed. The room wasn't as elaborate as I'd expected. The bed had a wooden headboard and the bedspread was simple white cotton tucked into hospital corners.

"Oof," Carmina grunted as she fell out of the chute and landed on the floor.

"'Bout time you made it," I said. The vampire's eyes flicked in her direction, and I raised an eyebrow at him to dare him to give me an excuse to fire.

"Who'd you shoot?" Carmina demanded.

"The wall."

"Um, Zed—"

As she came to join me, I spoke over her to the vampire, who watched us with an unblinking gaze. "Who are you?"

He shook his head, but I couldn't tell if it signified that he wouldn't tell me—or couldn't.

"Zed," she said.

Another shake of the head from the vampire.

"Maybe he's in the lab," I said, pointing to the door on the other side of the bedroom.

"Only Pontius Morordes may enter the lab." The vampire's voice sounded like rusty chains dragging along concrete.

"Do you know how to get in there?" I demanded.

The vampire tipped his chin to indicate he did.

"Zed, that's him," Carmina said with more force.

I didn't dare take my eyes from the vampire. "That's who?"

"Dr. Death."

I chanced a look at her face to see if she was joking. She didn't look amused. When I looked at the vampire again, he was still smiling, but he was also halfway around the bed toward us. "Don't move," I said to him. To Carmina, I whispered, "How do you know?"

"I know, okay? I knew him…before." She looked around for a moment, as if hoping proof might present itself. She finally walked toward the wall and pulled a picture from a hook to bring it to me. "Look, here's a photograph of him with the Prime. Trust me when I say the Prime isn't the kind of guy who has his picture taken with servants."

"Meridian Six?" the vampire hissed. "Is that you, my dear?"

Her face paled but she refused to look at him. "It's him." She walked across the room to check out the door, as if she needed space. The vampire's eyes followed her.

"There's a security pad here," she called. "How do we get in there?"

The vampire said nothing.

"Open it," I said.

"I do not take orders from humans."

I took a menacing step forward. "I will kill you if you don't."

The vampire smiled. "Please try."

"Is she right?" I asked the vampire. "Are you Pontius Morordes? Are you Dr. Death?"

Instead of answering, he lunged. One second

he was by the end of the bed, and the next Carmina flew across the room and a streak of gray slammed into me, knocking the gun from my hand. My body slammed backward into a side table that sent a lamp and other items crashing to the floor.

"Zed!" Carmina's shout was almost lost in the growls and hissing of the pissed-off vampire on top of me.

Dr. Death was slight in frame but not in temperament. He giggled as his hands closed around my throat and his fangs flashed like twin daggers in the low light.

His breath stunk of copper and his eye glowed with the sort of insanity only those truly genius possess. "The only way you're getting into my lab is as a test subject."

Black floaters swam in my vision as I gasped like a fish out of water.

Behind his head, Carmina appeared wielding a lamp, but before she could strike the vampire with it, he let go of my neck long enough to strike her and give me a few seconds of much-needed air. The lamp shattered on the ground and Carmina cried out in pain. Even though she was hurt, she didn't give up and came at him with her fists this time. This was my chance. If I didn't manage to dislodge him we'd both be dead soon.

I bucked with my hips at the same time I threw all my weight to the left. He fell toward the right and I managed to pull myself out from under him. Carmina immediately intensified her attack, swatted him with her fists like two pistons. Though my windpipe felt crushed and my neck throbbed, I pulled myself up to go help her.

The gun lay near the chute. Before I could reach it, Carmina screamed. I looked back in time to see the vampire's fangs sink into her forearm. The bastard growled and ripped a chunk out like a dog with a juicy bone. Carmina's skin went white and she fell, cradling the arm to her chest. I grabbed the gun and spun around.

The first bullet lodged in his shoulder. The impact knocked him back, but he stayed on his feet.

"Stop or the next one goes into your skull."

Carmina's blood smeared across his lips, which spread into a smile. "Your bullets don't scare me, human." As I watched in horror, he reached into the bullet wound in his shoulder and dug around until he pulled the slug out of the hole. He didn't even break a sweat. "The humans have a name for me, yes? Dr. Death." He chuckled. "It's precious, this name. Do you really think I'd have access to all of this technology and wouldn't formulate a way to become even stronger and more immune to your puny weapons?"

I pulled the trigger. The bullet exploded from the muzzle and drilled into the space between his eyes. His face exploded.

An instant later, Carmina started screaming.

CHAPTER 21

Meridian Six

The instant it happened, I felt as if I'd been shot. One second, Zed faced down Dr. Death while I waited for the right moment to attack. The next, Zed had done the one thing I'd explicitly asked him not to do.

When the gun fired and blood mist slapped against my skin, it took me a moment to comprehend what had happened. I screamed, not because I was afraid or sickened by the blood or the stench of copper. I screamed because it was better than attacking Zed.

"Carmina, hush." He grabbed my arms and shook me. I fought him off and went to check Dr. Death's pulse. Zed pulled me away. "Stop it. He's dead."

I fell back on the floor, not caring about the

blood and bone shards.

"Come on," he said. "We have to get out of here."

I wiped the blood from my face. "You said you'd give me the kill."

His mouth worked for a moment, as if he couldn't make sense of my words. "I had an opening, so I took it."

I looked him in the eyes. "You had no right."

He reared back as if I'd struck him. His expression hardened. "You weren't getting the job done."

The verbal jab hit home, but I wasn't ready to accept that if Zed hadn't been there, I'd be dead. "You didn't give me a chance. I was about to make a move. I just needed you to distract him for two more seconds." I stopped talking as the pressure of my frustration pushed against my ribs and made my head feel like it would shatter just as surely as the vampire's had. When word got back to Saga, he'd use this to trap me. He would use this as an excuse to back out of our agreement. He'd claim that since I hadn't dealt the deathblow that I'd broken our agreement. I looked at the terrible, bloody display beside me. There'd be more missions, each worse than the last. Each putting me one step closer to my own grave.

Zed ran his hands through his hair. "I don't get you. You—"

Something collided with the door that led out

to the corridor. Guards pounded the metal panel and shouted for Dr. Death.

Our conflict momentarily forgotten in favor of survival, Zed and I jumped up. "The lab," I said. "Quickly."

We ran to the panel opposite the one being worked on by the guards. Zed's bullet had fried the control box the guards were trying to access, but I didn't hold a lot of hope that they wouldn't find a way to manually bypass the system. The corresponding panel next to the lab door had lots of flashing buttons and a pad about the size of a palm.

"Do you think he was telling the truth about no one else being allowed to go in there?" Zed asked.

I punched a few buttons in a vain hope the door would magically open. "Maybe he has a card or something to open it." I jerked my head toward the body.

Zed shot me an annoyed look. I didn't give two shits about his feelings. He'd killed the guy— he could be the one to search his corpse. Without a word, he turned away to go inspect his pockets.

The pounding on the other door grew louder, as if they'd found a ram of some sort to batter against the metal. Now I knew how it would feel to be trapped inside a steel drum.

"Carmina." Zed raised his voice to be heard over the rhythmic pounding. "There's nothing."

Seconds pounded down in time with the

beating. I spun to look at the panel again. I touched the screen with the tip of my finger. Instead of pulling up a digital keypad as I'd expected, it flashed the words, "*Place palm in the designated area.*"

"Of course," I said.

"What?" Zed called.

Instead of answering, I walked over, ignoring the sound of the guards trying to get in and the large bulges in the door, and grabbed one of the dead vampire's hands. "Grab his other hand, but be careful—we need that one."

CHAPTER 22

Bravo

We were in luck. Dusk hung heavy on the horizon, but it wasn't quite full night, which meant the guard shift change hadn't happened yet. According to Matri, the human guards were mean, but they were also dumb.

The old lady led the way as the pair of us approached the guard station on the platform. Almost immediately, a guard I recognized from earlier in the week strolled out of his post and crossed his arms. "You aren't authorized to be here, Matri."

She hunched her shoulders, really playing up the helpless old lady thing, and shuffled forward. "My assistant was here earlier today to unload the trains and lost her ration card. We need to search the cars she worked in before the train leaves."

He laughed. "Dumb bitch."

"Please, she's new. She didn't know."

"What's in it for me, eh?" He raised a black eyebrow and ran his gaze over my body like an unwanted caress.

I tried to look meek, but it felt about as natural as wearing someone else's skin. "Please, I'll do anything." Matri had told me earlier that ration cards were more important than oxygen to the prisoners. The vampires didn't ration food for the workers. Instead, they used the system to control how much water prisoners could drink. If you misbehaved, water would be withheld. It was a clever system, since the human body could starve a lot longer than it could go without water. No doubt the asshole I was trying to bargain with had sold out his own species for access to all the fresh, cool water he could store in his belly.

"My shift is over in thirty minutes," he said. "Meet me behind the station and, if I like what you offer, I'll let you search the train."

The train's whistle blew.

"We don't have thirty minutes," Matri said. "By then the train will be long gone. Let her look now and she'll go with you after."

It took all my strength not to protest. I knew she was bluffing, but if our plan went wrong I'd have to go through with her promise or risk the guard turning us in.

"Let me have a sample now and you can go search."

Bile shot up the back of my throat. I started backing away, but Matri's surprisingly strong hand squeezed my arm.

"Just a taste," she said.

I realized then that I'd made the mistake of trusting a woman who'd survived by offering up children's veins to monsters. Of course she'd offer up my body, too, if it meant saving her own neck.

"Come on, then," the guard said, "give us a kiss."

"Back behind the building," Matri said. "If someone sees, we'll all be punished."

He nodded and walked around the side of the building farthest from the main entrance. Even though I knew sacrifices had to be made, I hadn't expected to be the lamb.

Matri shoved me forward.

"No," I gasped. "I don't—"

"Hush, girl," she hissed. "This is the only way."

I allowed her to push me after the guard, but inside, every cell in my body rebelled against what I was about to do.

When we reached him, he moved excitedly from foot to foot. Matri urged me toward him and his hand shot out to pull me in.

He smelled of cabbage and sweat. His feral smile revealed grayed teeth, before he flicked a pale tongue at me. I gagged and fought the inevitable. My resistance only seemed to excite him.

I'd never kissed a boy before. Zed was the only available candidate I'd known, but he was too much like a brother to consider sharing kisses. Now, under the cold stare of the guard's shark eyes, the idea that my first time would be with this human who'd betrayed his own people wasn't bearable.

"No." I pulled back, but ran into Matri's surprisingly solid body blocking my escape. The guard's hands tightened on my arm.

"No kiss, no ration card," he taunted.

Behind us, the train hissed and chugged impatiently. If I didn't hurry, the conductor would pull out of the station and we'd all be dead.

"Don't be a fool, girl," Matri hissed. "You'll kill us all."

I swallowed hard and licked my lips. The guard's eyes flared. He leaned in. Matri's hands urged me toward him. I didn't want this, but I couldn't be the reason the plan failed and we all died.

The instant I stopped resisting, my body slammed into the guard's chest. Before I could regain my equilibrium, his rough mouth found mine and that pale tongue slithered between my lips. I gagged but couldn't dislodge the invader. His hand clamped around my breast, and I whimpered against the pain.

Matri pulled me back and I stumbled out of the guard's grasp. "We promised you a sample and you've had it," she said.

The guard spat on the ground. "She better be more willing next time."

I gagged at the thought of allowing him to touch me again, but then I remembered that if things went according to plan I'd never have to see him again.

"She's a virgin," Matri said. "Whether she's willing or not, you'll have fun, yes?"

He chuckled. "Five minutes, no more."

Matri grabbed my arm and dragged me back to the platform. "Quickly," she urged me. "And wipe your tears."

I swiped at my eyes, more angry than afraid. "If this doesn't work, I am not going behind the station with him."

"Hush." She squeezed my wrist. "You'll do whatever is necessary to survive."

I wanted to tell her I wasn't like her. I'd never betray myself or anyone I cared about. But a voice in the back of my head wondered if being a martyr was better than living to fight another day. Either way, I didn't have time to debate morals with Matri.

While I'd been enduring my first kiss behind the station, Wu and Cleo had snuck the children and several other prisoners onto the train. Elsewhere, Tuck's people were placing dynamite throughout the camp. The plan was for them to catch up to the train before it crashed through the gates and the charges went off. When Tuck had agreed to the plan he'd had a weird little smile, like he was humoring us when he said he'd catch the train.

Wu waited for me on the platform. Matri ducked into one of the cars to check on the children, and I continued on with Wu toward the engine. According to Meridian Six, the train was engineered by a single vampire. Two human prisoners took turns shoveling coal into the engine.

I glanced back over my shoulder. The guard still hadn't come back around the corner, but wisps of smoke told me he was sneaking a cigarette while he waited for me to return. I shuddered and sped up.

The door to the engine was open, and shouts emerged from inside. "Hurry, hurry. We have to stay on schedule, maggots."

Wu and I exchanged a look. My hand itched for a weapon, but it had been too risky for me to carry one for my meeting with the guard. Luckily, Wu had a knife he'd made from the handle of an old comb. I resented being used as bait again, but Wu's size made him the smarter choice to be the killer.

At Wu's nod, I took a deep breath and stepped into the doorway. "Excuse me—"

I broke off as I took in the scene inside the engine. A short, round vampire in a conductor's cap had a hand raised as if to slap one of the two humans huddled in the corner by a large coal bin.

As one, all three turned to look at me.

"Who are you?" the vampire demanded.

"Excuse me, but the station master told me they needed to see you in the office before you go."

He lowered his hand slowly. "I got a schedule to keep."

I kept my posture meek and apologetic. "Sorry, sir, they said it was urgent."

He turned his back on the two humans and advanced toward me. Despite his small stature, his angry expression told me he had every intention of punishing me for interrupting the beating he'd meant for his prisoners. I glanced over his head at the pair. With their tormentor's back turned, they stood a little straighter. I raised my brows at them and prayed they understood the signal, but before I could move, the conductor's fist slammed into my belly.

I gasped and doubled over. The second blow landed on the side of my head.

"I told you I had a schedule to keep." More blows punctuated his words, but his voice remained calm, as if violence was simply a language to him, instead of the product of anger.

A blur of motion signaled Wu's arrival. He pushed me out of the way and went at the conductor with his makeshift knife. Male grunts and the wet sound of Wu stabbing the conductor's fat belly filled the engine.

"Start it up," Wu shouted.

I turned to the pair of prisoners. "Help me."

The stared at me blankly, as if they didn't understand the words. I shouted at them, "Coal, now!" The anger in my voice seemed to help them understand what I wanted. While casting curious glances at the fight, they scooped piles of coal into the firebox.

The engine's control panel lay before me like some sort of alien technology. Before the Blood Wars, humans got around on high-speed, electric trains run by computers. But once the vampires took over, they shunned most human technology, worried we might be able to take them over in the same way they had overthrown us. So it was back to basics with modified coal engines of their own designs. The panel in front of me didn't have any handy digital monitors with instructions. Instead a series of handles and knobs with no labels mocked me.

"Bravo," Wu yelled. "Any time now."

A glance over my shoulder revealed that Wu had the vampire pinned to the wall. The vamp's torso was a mural of bloody stab wounds, but he wasn't dead. He wouldn't die without his brain being destroyed somehow, and Wu's little knife couldn't get that job done. His only choice was to keep the vampire so wounded he couldn't stop us.

I grabbed one of the humans. He was taller than me, but backbreaking labor and starvation had wasted him to little more than skin stretched taut over bones. "How do I make the train go?"

His eyes were blackened, as if he'd withstood a recent beating. Those twin black holes blinked slowly at me. I shook him. "The train? How do I make it move?" I dragged him toward the panel. "Which one?"

He looked at the panel and back at my face. Maybe at one time he'd been a person with dreams and a family. Maybe he'd told jokes with his friends and laughed so hard his sides hurt. But now, the lights were on but the house was abandoned. I grabbed his arms and shook him. "Listen to me, if you help us, you'll be free. Understand?"

Behind us, the only sounds were the wet slurp of knife to open wound and the methodical whoosh of coal sliding into the furnace. The man next to me with the blackened hands and the empty eyes didn't move. In my gut, fear and frustration boiled over into rage. I slapped him, hard.

He didn't blink, he didn't shy away, and he didn't speak. I shoved him out of the way because I couldn't stand to look at him anymore. I should have felt guilty, but I didn't. Guilt could come later, when I had the luxury of a conscience again.

"Bravo, we're running out of time," Wu said.

"I'm on it," I snapped. Giving the panel all of my attention, I stared hard at each button and knob. None were labeled, of course, but after a moment I realized that one of the buttons was more worn down than all the others. I punched it and a loud hissing sound immediately filled the air. The prisoner pushed me out of the way.

"You're gonna make it explode," he said.

I was so shocked to hear him talk, I fell back out of his way.

He grabbed a lever and wound it several times. "The reverser," he said. He moved another lever. "Release the break and wait for the valve to reach enough pressure."

We both watched the valve reach twenty-one. He nodded. "Release the throttle. Easy, now, don't want to flood it with steam."

I nodded and released the throttle a couple of inches. The train lurched forward. I yelped from both surprise and excitement. "Thanks, uh, sorry, I don't know your name."

He smiled, revealing lots of gums but few teeth. "Stellen."

"Faster," Wu yelled. He'd stopped stabbing the vampire but still had his hands full holding him down.

I turned to my new ally. "How do we make it go fast?"

He rejoined his friend by the firebox and began shoveling again. With double the coal, the train gradually started moving faster, but nowhere near fast enough to barrel through the large gate looming a quarter mile ahead.

"More coal!" I called. "We have to get through the gates."

"It won't be enough," Stellen said. "We need more fuel. The coal takes too long to build speed."

"Any suggestions?" I asked.

He tipped his head toward the door. "Fat is fuel."

I gritted my teeth and turned to Wu. He raised his brow, leaving the final call up to me.

Suddenly, I realized I had a lot more in common with Matri than I'd expected. Because faced with my own death or making another person suffer, I took the easy road. "Throw him in."

CHAPTER 23

Zed

The lab looked like something out of a horror film. Corpses hung from hooks and were laid out on metal slabs. One whole wall bore shelves filled with body parts floating in colorful liquids. Along another wall, a row of dog-sized cages held the meek forms of prisoners too broken from pain to call for help.

Everything in me yearned to help them, but the sounds from the room we'd just fled indicated the guards had finally managed to break through the other door. If we didn't move quickly, we'd be praying for the luxury of dog kennels.

Carmina barely spared the prisoners a glance as she ran through the lab. She was mad at me, but I found myself struggling to feel guilty. Once we escaped—if we survived, that is—we had one hell of a fight waiting for us. But until that happened, we needed each other to survive, whether she liked it or not.

She reached the door on the far side of the lab and inspected the panel. "This one's easier," she said. "Just have to hit this button to open it."

"Wait," I whispered. "What if there are more guards out there?"

"You got a better suggestion?"

I pointed over the metal tables. A ventilation shaft hooked down from the ceiling. "That's got to lead to the top."

She glanced from the door to the shaft, and given her mood, I expected her to argue. But she must have come to the same conclusion I had about working together because she nodded. "Hurry." She ran and leapt onto the table. She was just tall enough to knock the vent cover off the tube. Her hair flew behind her as fresh air spilled out. "Give me a hoist, will ya?"

I joined her on the table and all but threw her up into the shaft. She didn't hesitate to pull me in after her. I pulled the vent cover up with me and and just got it snapped into place before the guards ran into the lab. We sat quietly as they ran to the other door and opened it. As I expected, a trio of guards rushed forward to meet them. As they shouted and argued, Carmina took the explosive Tuck had given us for the job and laid it beside the vent cover. She carefully pushed the button that would activate the timer. In ten minutes, the lab and everyone in it would be destroyed.

That done, we crawled as fast as we could through the tunnels to the outside. As we moved, I prayed that nothing delayed us on the way out or our ashes would spend the rest of eternity mingling with those of the monsters we'd come to kill.

It took three minutes to reach the ground floor of the building. The vent opened into a washing room. A couple of prisoners looked up from their work of sorting through laundry, but didn't react to seeing two humans crawl out of a ventilation shaft.

A human guard stood just outside an open door, smoking a cigarette. As we approached, his walkie-talkie let out a gasp of static. A voice shouted to be on the lookout for two prisoners. He turned down the volume and took another drag of his cigarette. It turned out to be his last.

Then we were running across the main plaza in front of the commander's building. On the large banner, Carmina's image watched us run for our lives.

On the far side of camp, the train's whistle shouted into the air. The clock in the center of the plaza showed it was two minutes after six.

"We're late," she yelled over her shoulder.

"Train's taking off late too. We can still make it."

We dug in and pumped our legs faster. Behind us, the sound of the prison alarm squawked over the loudspeakers. Ahead of us, the sun slipped below the horizon. The vampires in the bunkers below our feet woke from their sleep, and the first thing they'd hear upon rising was that the legendary Dr. Death had been murdered by two prisoners. There would be hell to pay. I just prayed that by the time they mustered themselves for the hunt, we'd be safely on that train.

"Faster," I shouted. "Faster!"

CHAPTER 24

Matri

"Faster, faster," I whispered, urging the train to gallop. We'd pulled from the station so slowly that the guard Bravo had kissed didn't even have to jog to keep up with our car as he shouted for us to halt. Luckily he didn't have a gun, nor enough to lose to try to jump onto the car. When he reached the end of the platform he spun and ran to the phone by the office door to call in reinforcements.

"Matri, where are we going?" The question came from the young that Bravo had arrived at the camp with. I looked into his round cheeks and wondered if he'd ever fully realize how lucky he was to have only been in Krovgorod for a couple of days instead of his whole life like the other children.

"Hush now," I said. "Go sit where I told you. It's not safe here by the door."

Cleo joined me once the young had done as I ordered. "We won't break through the gates without more speed."

"They'll manage it somehow, but for now let's hope the others catch us."

We were well beyond the station and moving along behind the storehouses and a few of the barracks. It wouldn't be long until we were in open space, where guards could line up their guns and shoot at will. The sun was slipping low and I prayed it would take the guards several precious minutes to organize themselves and get the weapons in line. If not, bullets would turn the cars into Swiss cheese before we even had a chance to make a decent run at those gates.

Our boxcar cleared the cover of the final building. In the distance, two figures ran from the promenade. Behind them, vampire guards swarmed out of the commander's building. On one hand, the sight was cause for celebration, because it meant Dr. Death was dead. On the other hand, it appeared that Zed and Carmina had managed to kick the hornets' nest on their way out. In addition to the guards chasing them, several armored cars zoomed out from behind the building, loaded down with vampires and mounted guns.

Even as I prayed they'd reach us in time, I also prayed that the train picked up so much speed they'd never catch us. The latter meant we'd have a better chance of knocking down those gates and Tuck's explosive surprise would give us a real chance at freedom. I didn't want Meridian Six or Zed to die, but I wanted to live. Bravo thought me selfish, but she was young yet.

The train suddenly lurched forward, as if they'd tossed a packet of dynamite into the firebox. I scrambled to grab hold of something, but I fell to the floor of the boxcar and bounced. My feet flew outside the car and I only just managed to grab the edge of the opening to avoid falling out completely.

"Matri!"

The children's worried cries couldn't penetrate the force field of blind panic. My upper body wasn't strong enough to pull myself back inside. My feet could only hang loose, because if I moved and they tangled in one of the train's wheels I'd be pulled under.

Cleo grabbed my wrists with her boiled lobster hands. She fell back on her rear end and tried to pull me back inside the train. The train rocked roughly. Cleo grunted and pulled, but couldn't get leverage. "Children, help!"

I felt like I was being stretched on Dr. Death's infamous torture rack. My shoulder sockets screamed and my legs burned from trying to keep them away from the train's wheels.

Small hands grabbed onto Cleo's shoulders and high cries punctuated the train's chugging progress. My chest scraped over the sharp edge. The pain was welcome because it meant I was moving in the right direction.

"Pull harder," Cleo shouted.

Another inch's progress.

Before I could feel too relieved, a loud *ping* sounded nearby. Three more followed close behind it.

"They're shooting," Cleo shouted. "Faster, children." She lurched back to try to pull me in further.

Bullets peppered the train. Wood shards and shrapnel bit into the skin of my legs and back. No part of me didn't hurt, and it was only a matter of time until those bullets found my flesh.

I closed my eyes and stopped grabbing onto Cleo's wrists. Either she'd lose her grip or I'd just slip out, eventually.

The first bullet ripped through my left calf. The hard pinch burst into a throbbing nebula of pain.

I don't know how long I just hung there, wracked with pain and waiting for the end. But suddenly the pressure on my wrists shifted and strengthened. "Damn it, hold on!"

When I opened my eyes, I saw Bravo looming over me. She squatted at the edge of the car, and had Cleo wrapped around her waist. "Just let me go," I begged.

Her eyes burned with the sort of conviction I'd lost years ago. "Don't you dare give up. Not now. Not after everything you've done to survive."

The weight of all of those decisions pulled me down. I'd convinced myself for years that I'd been trying to save the children as much as I'd been saving myself. But the truth simmered deep inside me. I stood by while the Troika hurt those kids because I knew that standing up to them would mean my immediate death. "Get the children away from the door and drop me, damn it!"

"You'll do no one any good as a martyr." She threw her weight back. My body jerked and my hips scraped over the threshold. As I slammed onto the floor, another bullet burrowed into my left thigh.

I screamed and my vision went spotty. Bravo wrapped her arms around me and we rolled. "Close the door," she screamed at Cleo.

As the door slammed home, cutting out all the light, I went limp from the pain. My left leg would be all but useless if I managed to survive the blood loss. "You should have let me die."

She whispered, "Too many have already been left behind."

I swallowed hard. Cold sweat covered my skin despite the fire in my leg. "Where'd you come from, anyway? Who's driving the train?"

"Wu's driving. I came back to check on you and see if I could help Six and Zed make it aboard." She released me and stood. "You're welcome, by the way."

I squinted up at her through the dim light. She looked like she'd aged five years since we'd first arrived at the station. "Thanks, kid."

She nodded and ran off without another word. As I watched her throw open the door leading to the caboose, I smiled despite my pain. If we survived this, she'd never let me forget how she'd saved my life, and damn me if I wouldn't feel grateful to her for giving me a second chance to make up for the things I'd done to survive.

As Cleo put pressure on my wounds, I closed my eyes and offered up whatever time I had left to fighting the good fight.

CHAPTER 25

Meridian Six

They were gaining on us. No matter how hard Zed and I ran, we'd never be able to outpace a vehicle. Even over the sound of my heart galloping in my ears, I could hear the roaring engines and the mechanical whining of the vampire's bat drones.

The train chugged down the track and gained speed with each passing second. We'd have to hustle even faster if we were going to make it. The only blessing was that the vampires had decided to aim their guns at it instead of us.

When we finally reached the track, Zed stumbled over one of the rails. I grabbed his arm and dragged him until he could regain his feet. Then we were running side by side toward the caboose. We'd almost reached it when Bravo burst through the rear door. She waved her hands wildly as if to encourage us to pick up speed. I kept my eyes trained on the two steps I had to climb before I'd be safely on the rear platform. The train was hustling, but hadn't gained full speed. Good news for us, but not so great for the plan to burst through the huge metal gates a bit farther down the track.

Zed fell back to let me go first. I dug in and pushed myself harder. My hand reached for the rail on the side of the metal steps. I got a fingertip on the metal but the train lurched forward out of my grasp. Cursing, I tried again.

This time I got two fingers around the rail. I pushed off the ground with everything I had and leaped onto the bottom step. My foot touched metal. I overcorrected to prevent myself from slamming into the next step. My body started to fall back. Panicked, my heart stumbled. Then a hand wrapped around my wrist and wrenched me forward.

I fell into Bravo but recovered quickly.

Without thanking her, I turned to see if Zed had made it yet. Red-faced and panting, he was almost there. I wrapped a hand around the rail and stood on the top step. I held out my free hand. "Come on!"

He extended his hand, brushing my fingers with his before losing the connection. I leaned forward as far as I could. "Hurry!"

Finally, he grabbed my hand and leapt. I held

my breath and pulled as hard as I could.

His body flew toward the bottom step. One foot made it. His expression opened up with hope. I grabbed and pulled before he could fall back.

Bullet sparked off the railing beside my head. That was all the encouragement we needed to scramble off the platform.

Just before I leaped inside the caboose, searing pain exploded in my right arm.

Then Zed was screaming and dragging me, and Bravo was pushing us into the caboose. Over their heads, I saw two motorcycles, each carrying vampires with big guns, gaining on us from the tracks.

I fell across the threshold into the dark car. The pain in my biceps robbed me of breath. Blood, lots of blood.

Zed ripped off his shirt and wrapped it around my arm, pulling it tight to cut off the blood loss. "Can you stand?"

I nodded. Seeing those vampires so close to the train released enough adrenaline to counteract the pain. "Two motorcycles, close," I gasped. "Need to get moving."

He looked like he wanted to tell me to sit down and rest, but we both knew we didn't have that luxury anymore. Instead, he turned to Bravo and took control. "How many people are on the train?"

"Wu's at the helm with two prisoners shoveling coal. We got fifty adults in the next car and twenty children in the one after. But the other cars I saw are full of supplies. Maybe if we dump some of it … "

Zed shook his head. "It'll take too long. We need everyone to move into the car closest to the engine. We can uncouple the rest faster than the time it'll take to dump stuff. I'll go warn Wu; you two get everyone to move forward. And hurry."

With that, he squeezed her arm, kissed my forehead, and took off toward the front of the train. In his wake, Bravo and I exchanged a look.

"He always that bossy?"

She laughed. "Hell, yes. You okay?"

I swallowed the nausea. Guess adrenaline couldn't totally erase the pain of a bullet wound after all. "I'll be fine. Let's hurry so we don't get left behind."

CHAPTER 26

Zed

When I finally burst through the door into the engine room, I found Wu at the controls and two humans I didn't recognize shoveling coal into the firebox.

Wu's greeting left something to be desired. "We're not going to make it."

"Yes, we are," I said. "Bravo and Carmina are moving everyone up so we can dump the other cars."

"It won't be enough." Wu pointed out the front window.

The gates were way closer than I expected. They were metal and looked strong enough to keep out a determined giant—or keep in a train of soul-weary prisoners.

"We should have had Tuck use that dynamite

on the gates," Wu said.

"That would have derailed us," I said. "Have a little faith, Wu."

The train surged faster. Bravo and Six must have begun uncoupling the cars as they progressed through the train. From my count, there were five more cars to go. I just hoped we had enough time to get the remaining four unhooked to get the speed we needed. There were only a couple with people, though, so hopefully it would go fast.

A loud explosion sounded far behind us. I ducked my head out to see a plume of smoke rise over the commander's building. Judging from the fire, it had caused a lot of damage. The bad news, of course, was all the guards it was supposed to kill were currently chasing the train.

Even as I had this thought, a motorcycle pulled even with the engine. I pulled Wu down just in time. A bullet cracked the glass of the train's front window.

"Damn it," Wu said. "We're going to need a miracle to pull this off."

"I don't know about you," I said, "but I lost my faith in the gods a long time ago. We'll have to pull this off without divine intervention."

The train sped up again. This time the increase was faster, which I hoped meant they'd gotten two cars unhooked at once. That only left one more.

"I'm going to go check on them."

"Hey, boy," Wu said.

I stopped at the door and raised my brows.

He tilted his head toward the looming gate. "When we crash through that thing, you better hold on to your ass."

I saluted him. "Yes, sir. You just make sure we stay on the tracks."

I let the engine room door slam behind me. In the gap between it and the next car, the wind whipped through, nearly dislodging me from the narrow platform. When I finally made it into the next car, the lack of wind was a huge relief, but it wasn't quieter there. Bodies crammed into the car like sardines in a can.

"Carmina! Bravo!" I yelled, but my voice was swallowed by the panicked whine of the children and the cries of men and women. The sound of bullets against the side of the car created a nerve-wracking rhythm, a sensation only heightened by the claustrophobia of all those unwashed bodies in the tight space.

I pushed through the crowd as fast as I was able. Eventually, I made it to the other end only to find the rear door open and even more bodies coming through. A man standing by the opening helped people across the gap between it and the next car.

"Where's Bravo? Carmina?"

He shrugged. "Don't know them." Then he dismissed me because he needed to help a woman carrying a toddler across. I waited for that pair to make it before leaping over to the other car myself.

A handful of people crowded near the next door with Bravo at the front. She grabbed my hand to pull me across. "Where's Carmina?" I shouted over the rushing wind.

She pointed back over her shoulder.

I leaned in. "We need to hurry. We're almost at the gates."

She nodded and pushed me back to get busy. "All right everyone, faster now."

The people behind her parted to allow me into the car before resuming their exodus.

Carmina leaned against a wall. Her right arm was a bloody mess. She was so pale and weak that she looked like a ghost of herself. I rushed over to her.

"Hey, come on. We need to get you across."

She shook her head. "They're almost done anyway."

"We're almost at the gate. We need to hurry." I urged her toward the doorway. Bravo was already helping the last person across.

Carmina allowed me to get her closer to the opening. She leaned heavily on my side.

Bravo leaped over the opening and turned for me to hand Carmina over.

I looked to the side in time to see us pass the guard tower just in front of the gates. On the front, another banner with Meridian Six's smiling face mocked me. Time was up.

I looked up at Bravo. "Uncouple it."

She shook her head.

I pushed Carmina across the opening. Bravo was so busy catching her, she couldn't stop me from swooping down to hit the mechanism to unhook the cars.

A hiss sounded.

The car pulled away from the one where Bravo and Carmina watched with growing horror as I fell behind.

I reached out a hand to wave goodbye.

CHAPTER 27

Meridian Six

After Bravo caught me and I turned to see Zed messing with the coupling, a spurt of anger and adrenaline transformed me.

As he raised a hand to wave goodbye. I jumped forward and grabbed his wrist.

For a heart-stopping moment, gravity captured me and pulled me toward the blurry ground.

But then hands clamped around my waist and my body went taut from the opposing forces—Bravo and the others pulling me toward the train and Zed's arm stretching as he fought to dislodge my grip.

"No!" he shouted. "Let me go!"

His eyes widened as he stumbled forward off the retreating car. I fell to the platform at the back of the train and he fell toward the ground.

Bravo and the others hauled us backward. Zed's eyes went wild from fear as his legs kicked uselessly against the air.

The arms around my waist made breathing difficult. Zed's wrist slipped a fraction of an inch in my hand. Moving my injured arm was torture, but I needed to give him something to grip. He took a quick look at the wrist I offered him, clenched his jaw, and grabbed on. White fire shot up my arm and the pain made me gag.

The bodies behind me pulled all their weight backward. I sobbed freely and screamed my rage.

It wasn't right.

None of this was right.

Even though I'd grown up in the Troika's bleak world, I couldn't believe we'd get this close to freedom only to die at the gates. But I also knew that if we didn't get Zed inside and brace ourselves, the train's collision would kill us all.

"Bravo!" I shouted. "On three, we all fall back."

"Three," was all she said. Behind me, I heard the word echo down the line.

"One." I planted my feet on the ground.

Zed tightened his grip.

"Two." I bent my knees.

He looked up into my eyes, his own hard with determination, and nodded.

"Three!" I flew backward.

Something slammed into my front. Cushion of bodies braced us from behind.

The terrible scream of metal on metal. Bodies flung around. Gravity reversing and then doubling. Pain everywhere.

But then, a miracle. Despite the pain and the echoes of screaming, the train continued to move forward.

I peeled open my eyes to see through the open rear door. The gates, now bent and twisted, grew smaller in the distance. Something solid moved underneath me. I looked down to see Zed's face, his expression dazed and filled with pain.

"Are we dead?" he groaned.

I lifted a trembling hand to point to the rectangle of light. "Look."

I rolled off him and we crawled together to look.

He took my hand as we watched the prison's walls grow smaller behind us. Unfortunately, we also saw vampires crawling over the rubble of the ruined gates to give chase.

"They won't stop coming," he said. "Tuck's dynamite didn't wor—"

A tidal wave of heat and sound launched us backward. By the time we recovered and pulled ourselves upright, the entire camp had erupted into a series of fireballs.

A cheer rose up in the crowded car.

Zed and I exchanged astonished looks. My entire body felt like a wound, but I'd never felt better in my life. We'd done it.

I don't know who moved first, but next thing I

knew we'd fallen into each other. We sort of just collapsed together, holding up each other's weight, as we'd held each other up throughout the entire rescue.

"I'm sorry," he whispered into my ear.

I shook my head against his shoulder. "Don't worry about it."

"But killing him was your ticket, right?"

I pulled back to look at him in shock. "How'd you know?"

He looked sheepish. "I told you, I eavesdropped that night."

"It doesn't really matter. I was a fool to think Saga would honor any agreement. Now that we've managed this victory he'll only double his efforts to use me as the poster girl for the rebellion."

"Of course it matters. I saw those posters. You've never not been used by someone. First it was the Prime and now it's Saga and Icarus, right?"

My eyes stung, but it had nothing to do with pain or the smoke from the explosions. "Saga would be a fool not to use me—us, actually—as symbols to encourage other humans to rise up. I get it. I really do. I just wish—Well, what I wish doesn't matter much, does it? As long as the Troika is in power none of us will ever really be free."

Zed looked back over all of the people in the car. They were hugging and crying openly. His gaze lingered on Bravo and the kid we'd gone to save.

"We could run away."

I frowned at him. "What about your youngs?"

"Bravo will look after them. And Matri." He nodded toward Matri and Bravo, who were hugging. I'd noticed tension between the women when I first met them, but I guess all of that got sorted out sometime between then and almost dying. I glanced at Zed. Funny how almost losing everything realigned one's priorities.

"We can help dig Tuck and the others out of the mines and then sneak off to make our own way."

I thought about all of those hopeless faces. The humans who'd been imprisoned in this labor camp. There were others—more camps, more prisoners, more tragedies waiting to happen. How could I run away knowing there was so much work left to be done? I'd spent so much time longing for my own freedom as some sort of payment for the ills I'd suffered, but there were so many others who needed help.

"Thanks for the offer, but running away isn't my style." I squeezed his hand. "I don't think it's yours, either." And that was one of the things I liked most about him.

"But—"

I shook my head. "I don't love Saga and Icarus's methods, but that doesn't mean they're wrong about needing to overthrow the Troika or the role I need to play in that. Before I came on this mission, I was ready to walk away and never look back. But now?" I looked around the car at each face, once so bleak, barely more than walking corpses. Now, for the first time in years, they were smiling, daring to hope for their future.

I smiled at Zed through tears of my own. "Now, I understand that this is worth fighting for."

He tilted his head and squeezed my hand.

When he kissed me, it was soft and quick, a promise instead of a demand.

And for the first time in my life, I allowed myself to hope for my own future.

ACKNOWLEDGEMENTS

Many thanks to Timons Esaias for offering his critical eye to a large portion of this novella. In addition, early chapters of this story were workshopped with the help of Will Horner and several of my Seton Hill MFA cohorts, including Kourtnea Hogan, Lynn Hortel, TJ Lantz, Chase Moore, Alex Savage, and Tanya Twombly. Much gratitude to Heather Osborn for her excellent developmental edits. Any technical errors or lapses in logic that made it into the final product are solely mine.

ABOUT THE AUTHOR

Jaye Wells is a USA Today-bestselling author of urban fantasy and speculative crime fiction. Raised by booksellers, she loved reading books from a very young age. That gateway drug eventually led to a full-blown writing addiction. When she's not chasing the word dragon, she loves to travel, drink good bourbon and do things that scare her so she can put them in her books. Jaye lives in Texas.

Connect with me online:
Twitter: http://twitter.com/JayeWells
Facebook: https://www.facebook.com/AuthorJayeWells
Web site: http://www.JayeWells.com

Printed in Great Britain
by Amazon